❧ The Whirlwind ❧

The Whirlwind

Carol Matas

ORCA BOOK PUBLISHERS

Library and Archives Canada Cataloguing in Publication

Matas, Carol, 1949-
The whirlwind / written by Carol Matas.

ISBN-13: 978-1-55143-703-3
ISBN-10: 1-55143-703-1

I. Title.

PS8576.A7994W47 2007   jC813'.54   C2006-906393-1

First published in the United States, 2007
Library of Congress Control Number: 2006938764

Summary: Ben flees Nazi Germany only to find himself in a
battle for his life and his soul.

Orca Book Publishers gratefully acknowledges the support for its publishing
programs provided by the following agencies: the Government of Canada
through the Book Publishing Industry Development Program and the Canada
Council for the Arts, and the Province of British Columbia through the BC
Arts Council and the Book Publishing Tax Credit.

Design and typesetting by Christine Toller
Cover art direction by Doug McCaffry
Cover artwork by Gary Alphonso
Author photo by Ruth Bonneville

ORCA BOOK PUBLISHERS
PO Box 5626, STN. B
VICTORIA, BC CANADA
V8R 6S4

ORCA BOOK PUBLISHERS
PO Box 468
CUSTER, WA USA
98240-0468

www.orcabook.com
Printed and bound in Canada
Printed on 100% PCW paper.

10 09 08 07 • 4 3 2 1

For my new granddaughter,
Naomi Jessi Nathanson
With love from your Savta

Acknowledgments

I'd like to thank all those who helped me with my research: especially, in Seattle, Ernest Stiefel, Doris Stiefel, and the Washington State Jewish Historical Society, as well as Michele Yanow from NextBook, who led me to the Stiefels; and in Vancouver, Marcy Babins and Diane Rodgers of the Jewish Historical Society of BC, and Frieda Miller of the Vancouver Holocaust Education Centre. Many thanks to Perry Nodelman, who read the manuscript numerous times and always came back with insightful advice, and to my daughter Rebecca, who only needed to read three pages of a draft to know immediately what wasn't working.

Thanks to my editor, Sarah Harvey, for her insights, editorial expertise and support. And thanks to the Manitoba Arts Council for the grant that gave me the time to write the book. And finally, thanks to my husband, Per, who drove me all the way from Winnipeg to Seattle to Vancouver and back to Winnipeg. And who allowed me to use his poems in this book.

Chapter One

Seattle, June 1942

I sit on the cold floor in the empty house and I wonder—did I get it all wrong? I feel like I'm in the middle of a whirlwind. Not a whirlwind of snow or dust or rain or wind, but one made up of tiny pieces of film that have been sliced up and thrown into a vortex; the swirling mass circles me and circles me and I see little bits of my life, but I can't quite make sense of it, can't quite put it all together to make a nice, neatly wound roll.

A cat screeches outside and I jump up, startled. I peer out the window. I pace across the wooden floor. It creaks.

I need to go back over it all. I need to grab the little pieces and try to see them, try to hear them, try to understand.

The first fragment is from years ago. It's me and my teacher, Mrs. Grundfeldt, on November 14,

1938—three and a half years ago. I remember the
date because it was my birthday. I was turning
eleven, and I was waiting to see what my cousin
Elizabeth was going to give me at recess. My
eyes were on the clock. That's all I was thinking
about.

"Benjamin Friedman. Stand up!"

I jumped.

"Yes, Mrs. Grundfeldt?"

"You will leave class now. And do not return."
She was sitting in her chair, her arms folded, her
thick eyebrows knitted almost together, her huge
bulk leaning slightly forward.

"But why?"

"You are a Jew. From now on," she paused
before she delivered the next words, her voice full
of satisfaction, "no Jews will be allowed to attend
school anywhere in Germany." She slapped the
desk with her big hands.

For a moment what she said just didn't sink in.
Then she repeated it. "All Jews are being thrown
out of school so as not to contaminate the rest of
us with their diseases and their bad ideas. Did you
hear me, Benjamin?"

Slowly I got up from my desk. I heard her, but
despite everything that had already happened—
Father and Mother being chucked out of their
university posts, Oma and Opa being fired—I
never thought they'd go after us children. I
looked around the room, desperately scanning it

for something—anything—that would let me get back at her. I noticed her favorite plant, a red begonia she fussed over so it would flower constantly. It sat on a small table by the door. I walked straight over to the plant, took a deliberate swipe at it and knocked it over. Dirt spilled onto the floor.

"Benjamin!" Mrs. Grundfeldt shrieked.

"What are you going to do, Mrs. Grundfeldt?" I replied, glaring straight at her. "Send me to the office? I am no longer a student here."

I shoved the entire pot onto the floor. It landed with a crash, crushing the flower. I opened the door, stalked out, then slammed it behind me. I didn't allow myself to cry.

Outside the building the other Jewish students in the school, probably a hundred or so, including Elizabeth, were milling around; no one wanted to leave because we knew it would be forever.

"So," Elizabeth said to me. "Now what?"

"We have a holiday," I answered. "Want to go to the conservatory? It is still my birthday," I reminded her.

"Don't you ever get sick of looking at plants?" she asked.

"You know the answer to that," I answered.

So we went, and she gave me my present there—a small cutting of an African violet. None of us had any money by then, and I thought it was a terrific gift. I tried to concentrate on its small beauty, instead of Mrs. Grundfeldt's hatred.

Elizabeth was over one evening for dinner when Father asked her what she wanted to be when she grew up.

"I want to be a poet," she answered.

Father nodded in approval. "You'll have to study hard."

"I know," she said. "I'm not afraid of hard work." Then she added, "But Hitler might finish me before I get a chance."

"Two Jews made a plan," Mother said. "They would assassinate Hitler. They found out that he drove past the same corner at the same time every day, so they waited for him, guns hidden. At exactly two o'clock they were ready to shoot, but he didn't arrive. Ten minutes later, still no Hitler. Half an hour later one of the men said, 'Dear me, I certainly hope nothing has happened to him!'"

We both laughed. Elizabeth was always laughing. "I have a funny story too," Elizabeth said. "It's about what Ben and I used to do at school to the teachers. We had competitions," she explained as I motioned frantically at her to be quiet, "to see who could play the best pranks and get away with them. I always won," she boasted. "Ben always got caught. Once he put a live frog on Herr Messinger's desk and got caught in the act. I put butter on Frau Gruding's door handle so she couldn't open it, and she was stuck in her room for ages. Of course I got away with it. And I put a beetle in Herr Mellor's sandwich. He hates bugs. It was so funny to watch him scream and then try to pretend he hadn't."

Thankfully Mother and Father were so fond of Elizabeth and so angry with the school for expelling us that they didn't get upset but actually found the whole thing funny. I think Elizabeth needed to be around people who could laugh and just have some fun; her mother, Irene, my mother's sister, was such a quiet person, nose always in a book.

After dinner, Elizabeth read me a new poem. She tried to write one a week. I was her favorite audience because I liked everything she wrote. Sometimes I'd read them over and over until I'd memorized them and could recite them back to her. That night the poem went something like:

Time flows faster than a river of tears
still it is steadfast as rock.
If you rest your head on it angels can be
heard building another day.

I was just leaving school—one run by the Jewish community in a synagogue—when a mob led by Brownshirts swarmed up and smashed all the stained glass windows. I slipped behind a tree just in front of the iron railing. I couldn't move or they'd see me. A group of them ran into the synagogue. Next thing I knew they were dragging Rabbi Wolf out to the pavement. He had a new baby and had brought her to class a couple of days earlier to show her off. About a dozen of them forced him to lie on his stomach, face on the concrete. Then they brought the Torahs out. They pulled him up. One of them, very young, face covered in acne, ordered him to light the match that would burn the Torahs. He refused. They beat him. And beat him. And beat him. Then they threw him in a truck and took him away.

He had been so brave. But I had hidden, too terrified to show my face, too paralyzed by fear to help him.

I crept home after they took him away, slipping from doorway to doorway. The mob was throwing stones into the windows of all the Jewish shops. They dragged any Jews they could find into the street and beat them or arrested them.

The newspapers the next day called it the Night of Broken Glass—*Kristalnacht*. Father was sure the entire world would wake up and tell Hitler and his goons to stop and we'd finally be safe, but *Kristalnacht* didn't wake up anyone. The world was asleep. The world didn't care about Jews. We were all alone.

Chapter Two

"Ben, you can't take the plants with you!" Mother reiterated.

"Most of them are just cuttings," I said, "and Elizabeth gave me this African violet for my birthday years ago."

"Don't you think they'll have cuttings in Seattle? You've seen pictures. It's full of flowers." She paused. "Leave the past behind, Ben."

I put the cuttings on the floor and continued packing. I wanted to leave Berlin with the clothes on my back and nothing more. "None of this is worth taking," I muttered.

"Just pack enough to tide you over while we travel," Mother advised. And then she went into Marta's room to argue with her. I could hear Marta say, "But I have to take my dolls. I can't leave them here!" and Mother's voice murmuring firmly in reply.

It's about time. That's all I could think. Why had Father waited so long? Opa had been begging him for years to get us all visas, but Father didn't believe in running away. If a train were coming right toward him, he'd probably stand his ground. Finally, *finally*, when it became clear that Hitler's campaign against the Jews was not going to pass, Father started the application process with the help of a good friend in the visa office.

"Papa's taking *his* books!" Marta's voice echoed through the almost-empty apartment. Our furniture had long ago been sold to get money for food. It wasn't even our apartment anyway. We'd been forced out of our home and into a cramped flat; no Jews were allowed to keep their property.

"Papa won't be able to find those books in America," Mother replied. "Now hurry—we need to see Opa and Oma off at the train station."

Since Oma and Opa couldn't get visas, they were going to stay in the country at their cottage. Although it too had been taken away from them and given to a non-Jew, at least the new landlord, the owner of the local pub, knew them well and had agreed to let them stay for a bit. They hoped they might slip through Hitler's net somehow.

I had trouble imagining life without them. I was used to seeing Oma at least a few times a week. We'd go over the latest cuttings, grafts and new shoots that she always had in her small greenhouse. Since I was little she had taken me with her on her jobs—creating and planning gardens for houses, government buildings or private contractors—

until being a Jew meant she could no longer work. But she kept the greenhouse at her apartment, and when she and Opa were forced to move, she managed to take a small part of it with her. When I was there, it seemed as if nothing bad was happening in the world. All around us were the flowers and plants she coaxed to grow and thrive. Even after Opa was beaten up one day by the Brownshirts and his health weakened, even then she always found time for her plants. I hoped she'd be able to concentrate on her garden in the country, but deep down I knew that there was nowhere for a Jew to hide in Germany. Part of me wondered if they were only going to the cottage so Father wouldn't feel so bad about leaving them behind. Maybe they worried that he might change his mind and not go at all. Above all, they wanted us to get out.

Oma and Opa were dressed in their summer best, even though it was years old and Oma had ladders in her stockings. Still, she wore a hat and gloves, and Opa wore his summer suit with a straw boater. Oma gave me a package with some seeds in it. "It's small," she said, "and you should be able to take it with you in a pocket of your pants. And when you plant them, you'll think of me and Opa." Her normally white skin looked even paler than usual, if that was possible, and her blue eyes glinted, almost as if she was in some kind of physical pain, trying to hold back the tears.

I took the packet from her, put my arms gently around her thin back and hugged her. "I'll think of you no matter what," I whispered.

"And I you," she said, drawing back and holding me by the shoulders, her grip firm. "Be happy, Ben. But remember. Our people elected Herr Hitler. A country gets the leaders it deserves. Never forget that. It can happen anywhere. Work to make sure it doesn't happen again. Promise?"

"I promise," I said.

"And be happy, Ben. Be happy. Don't let this horror snatch your happiness away. Life is short. There is joy in the world. There is," she said fiercely. And then she turned away from me to hide her tears.

I gave Opa a hug too, and he hugged me back so tight I almost cried out. As was his way, he didn't say anything. He hoped he could be of some use as a doctor where they were going, but even then I think we all knew that was unlikely to happen.

As we left the station I was so full of anger at Father it was all I could do to hold my tongue. Mother would be unable to bear the pain if I began to argue with Father at that moment. But it was all so obviously his fault; had he done as Opa had asked, we could have all gotten out together. As it was, his friend at the visa office wasn't able to help Oma and Opa at all.

‹‹ ››

Saying good-bye to Elizabeth was just as hard. We hardly knew what to say to each other, so we sat in the near-empty flat not speaking until she blurted out, "You know I still don't think you should leave. Things will get better, especially if we're sent away to the east for resettlement. And what if you have trouble fitting in, in Seattle?"

"Why should I?" I countered. "My English is excellent, thanks to Father."

"It's not all that perfect," she said.

"I can translate anything," I told her.

"Fine," she answered, looking around the room. Father had left his Reform Bible on the mantel. Elizabeth grabbed it, opened it at random and pointed. "Translate this."

I looked. "The book of Job?"

"If you're so smart."

"Fine," I agreed. "I will."

We stood there for a moment, me staring at the Bible because I couldn't bear to look at her, until Elizabeth stood on her tiptoes, kissed me on the cheek, turned and ran out of the flat. I stood there for ages, thinking about what I would do to Hitler if I could get near enough to hurt him. Would I kill him slowly or would I just put a bullet through his head?

I checked my watch as we left the station—it was exactly 10:46 AM on July 4, 1941. Even though I couldn't wait to leave, I was still angry, upset and even anxious that someone might yet stop us. To take my mind off the fact that we were leaving the city I'd grown up in—probably forever—I took the Bible out of my knapsack and turned to the book of Job. Father noticed what I was doing and asked me the reason.

"Elizabeth dared me to translate it into English," I replied.

"Job?" Father asked, perplexed.

"Yes," I said. "So I will. At least it will give me something to do on the trip. And it will help me practice my English."

Father looked dubious. "It's a troubling piece," he said. "Not really the thing to be reading right now." He paused. "But if you like, I could help you."

I thought about his offer for a minute. If I accepted, he might think I had forgiven him. Since saying good-bye to Oma and Opa, I'd barely spoken a word to him. On the other hand, the translation would be complicated, and he could help me understand what I was translating, which wasn't cheating, was it? I had told Elizabeth that I would mail her what I'd done, so I couldn't really get out of it.

"All right," I agreed.

He nodded. He tried not to show it, but I could tell that he was pleased. He used to be a professor of English at Hombolt University. Mother taught there as well—mathematics. That's where they had met as students. They'd both been teaching at the Jewish school since Marta and I started going there. I supposed that translating Job from the German would present an interesting challenge to an English scholar and keep him busy too.

We read the prologue and I could see right away why Father was reluctant to study it. He reminded me that Reform Jews like us don't believe that the Bible is the literal word of God—but it was still a strange story. Job is happy and prosperous and loves God. God points Job out to Satan and boasts about what a good man he is. Satan says he doubts that Job would be so good if he lost everything; he would certainly curse God, not praise Him. So God and Satan agree on a bet to see how Job will react. Satan strips Job of everything, starting with killing his children! Satan follows that with taking away all Job's worldly goods. When Job refuses to curse God, Satan goes after him again, covering him in boils from head to foot. And God lets him do all this—His only stipulation is that Satan mustn't kill Job.

By the time we'd translated the prologue, the day was over and I dropped into an uneasy sleep, plagued by nightmares of an angel named Satan leading a group of Brownshirts who attack Opa. I woke up in a sweat at some point and looked out the window into the night. Everything seemed so ordinary. Lights flickered in the darkness. People were probably doing ordinary things like

brushing their teeth before bed or reading a good
book, the sheets thrown off because of the heat.
The train chugged on with its soothing motion.
In some ways it was so ordinary that I wasn't sure
what was dream, what was reality, what was nightmare, what was truth.

Chapter Three

We crossed the German-Lithuanian border, transferred to a Russian train later that night and arrived in Moscow the next morning. I felt such a relief to be away from Germany, but I didn't think I would really feel secure until I was on American soil. A skinny young Jewish fellow with bug eyes and a tiny mustache proudly took us on a tour of Moscow, including the brand-new subway station decorated with statues of Lenin and Stalin; a day of propaganda, Father called it.

We were a whole week on the Trans-Siberian Express. The food was miserable, so fatty that everyone got sick. The bathrooms were overused and disgusting and there was nothing interesting or exciting to do. Father had brought a copy of *The Three Musketeers* for me and a copy of *The Secret Garden* for Marta, and we just immersed ourselves in our books. Finally we reached Manchuli, Manchuria. We were able to get off the train for a day and walk around and that felt like heaven. That night we caught a train to Harbin in Inner Mongolia. We had to change trains there and the station was a nightmare. Raw meat, covered in flies, was displayed everywhere. The flies swarmed all over us, even into our eyes, and, of course, ruined any appetite we might have had. Fortunately we were only there for a few hours until we caught the next train to Pusan in Korea, where we were to catch a boat to Japan.

I thought the boat would be fun, but half the group became seasick. I was fine. So was Marta, but Mother and Father didn't fare as well and were very happy to put their feet on dry land again. We stayed in Kobe, Japan, for two whole days with a friend of Father's brother. We slept on mattresses on the floor and ate very strange-tasting food: raw fish and rice with something called soy sauce. Finally we started on the last part of the journey— third-class passage on the *Hikawa Maru*, bound for Seattle by way of Vancouver. We arrived on Vancouver Island in Canada on July 22, and then we went on to Vancouver. We were so close to freedom now, I could feel it in the very air.

I gazed at the beauty around me and really couldn't believe my eyes: the mountains, the setting sun and the green forest beyond. We weren't allowed off the ship, though, because Canadian officials said we were Enemy Aliens. We were stuck there for two whole weeks while US Immigration came aboard to clear us before letting us travel on to Seattle. Our papers were scrutinized over and over and over. I was sure something was going to go wrong at the last moment and that we'd be sent back, but the local Jewish community intervened and at last we cleared US Immigration and continued on to Seattle.

As we pulled into port in Seattle, gulls swooped around the ship, the water sparkled in the sun, and the city seemed to gleam with golden light.

When we got off the boat, some men kissed the ground. I felt like doing it too, but I was too embarrassed to put on such a display. Still, my heart was soaring just like the gulls overhead. And there was Uncle Isaac—our sponsor and the only reason we had been able to immigrate. I hadn't seen him since I was little. I knew that he was nothing like Father, though, in looks or personality. He's short and stocky, whereas Father is tall and thin, although they have the same curly brown hair and brown eyes. Isaac dropped out of school young and went to work, traveled all over the continent and finally left for America.

He took us home right away to his apartment, where we'd be living squeezed in with him. It was situated over the furniture shop he owned. I liked the shop right away. It was full of gleaming wood furniture—chests, beds, tables, mirrors, lamps, wardrobes, coat stands—and all sorts of little knickknacks. Uncle Isaac offered to take us for a walk around the neighborhood and Father quickly agreed. We were all so happy to be free, to be able to walk outside without fear, to breathe the air; such simple things, but denied to us in Germany. And it was so pretty! The houses in the area were perched on hills. Lovely green lawns led up to freshly painted white exteriors; flower beds brimmed over. I noticed daisies, lavender, cosmos, peonies, many different roses and lots of other plants that Oma would have known the names of right away.

I was huffing and puffing and covered in sweat by the time we got home—being unable to exercise as we traveled had obviously not helped my chubby frame. Uncle Isaac fed us corned beef sandwiches on rye bread with pickles, and chocolate ice cream for dessert. Everything tasted perfect to me. After we'd eaten, Marta and I went to the room we were to share, a small room with a small bed on each side. Small but all ours. I lay down in my own bed, in my family's own house in America, and I fell asleep almost happy.

On our first full day in Seattle I noticed that Uncle Isaac often slipped into the back room of the shop to confer with his "associates." He put Father to work in the front of the shop. One of Uncle Isaac's associates was a skinny little guy with red hair who talked so fast I couldn't follow his English at all, and I had thought my English was excellent. The other was a dark-haired fellow with a nose that looked like it had been broken a few times. He spoke Yiddish, which is close enough to German that I was able to understand him without too much trouble. I wondered what they did back there. I imagined that maybe they were gangsters with big machine guns and that everyone in Seattle had to obey them or else.

I happened on Uncle Isaac and his two friends one afternoon when they were sitting with five other men around a table playing cards. Uncle Isaac pulled me aside. "Hey, kid, we don't want your father involved with this. He wouldn't approve."

"With what?" I asked.

"A little gambling operation I have."

I nodded. "Don't worry, Uncle Isaac," I said. "I won't tell."

"Good boy."

Father would try and stop him if he knew about the gambling, but I figured having a few toughs around was a good thing. It actually made me feel safer. I was a little disappointed that they weren't gangsters—that might have been better. Cards and gambling were pretty tame compared to what I'd been imagining. In some ways I would have preferred to be with them than go to school, because they could probably teach me how to be tough, which would be more useful than learning math.

« »

I stood awkwardly at the front of the class that first day of school. I'd been put into eighth grade instead of ninth because my birthday was in November and my English was not quite perfect. I didn't mind.

"Would you like to share my desk?"

I looked over to see a thin boy, medium height with dark eyes—quite the opposite of me, so tall and so heavy. He smiled.

I smiled back.

"Thank you."

"Please." He motioned me to sit. He looked Japanese, but he didn't have an accent.

He didn't say anything else. He asked me no questions—not one—and made no conversation until after school as we were leaving class.

"My name is John Ogawa. Would you like to walk with me?"

"Yes," I replied, surprised and pleased by the friendly gesture.

There was no chatting as we walked. He politely invited me back to his house, though, and I accepted. It was a white two-story with a big beautiful garden in front. His parents and both his brothers were at home, and when we walked in the door, formal introductions began.

"Mother, Father, this is Ben Friedman." Mr. Ogawa made a small bow, and then Mrs. Ogawa did the same. I wasn't sure what to do, so I bowed as well. "These are my older brothers, Michael and Frederick." They shook hands with me in turn. Mrs. Ogawa smiled. "Will you stay and have dinner with us?" she asked. "You are very welcome."

"Thank you." When I asked to call my parents, they showed me the phone and I made the call as quickly as possible, even though Mother wanted to ask me all sorts of questions.

Dinner was delicious: fish and rice with soy sauce on everything. No one asked me anything. They just let me eat in silence. It was wonderful.

The minute I returned home, though, Mother had to know exactly where I had been. When I told her, she asked what the family was like, what John was like, how school had been, was the teacher nice. I tried to answer everything with one word for each question, a word like "fine" or "good." Why do mothers need to know every detail of your life?

Later that night Father said, "Tonight we'll discuss another chapter of Job."

I had gotten sick of discussing Job early on in the trip and would have given up, but Father doesn't believe in giving up. He said I needed to finish what I'd started. "I don't want to discuss," I replied.

"We'll discuss. You cannot learn if you do not discuss."

Marta interrupted. "Ben, wasn't school fun today? Did you see me playing baseball? I was chosen third today. I'm going to be very good. By next year, in seventh grade, I'll be on the official team, I bet! A real American!"

I told Father I had too much homework to do, so he couldn't argue with me about Job. And I really did have homework. I wanted to do well at school and be respected. I didn't even mind studying that night because I, like Marta, was hoping to be a real American soon.

We'd had no word at all from Oma and Opa, but I finally got a letter from Elizabeth. It was short. She wrote that all Jews had to sew yellow stars on their clothes and that simply going out had become terribly dangerous because anyone could see who was a Jew and who wasn't. She said that they'd been given notice that they would be moved in a few days—so probably by the time I got the letter she'd been shipped out of Germany. But where to? I tried not to think about what it could mean. And why had we heard nothing from Oma and Opa?

Elizabeth included a new poem on a separate piece of paper. I must have read it a hundred times that night.

*On this road grass sprouts in the cracks
and pebbles lie loose. Treading must be done
softly in bare feet and if you're lucky enough
to wear shoes, it won't be for long.
There's an even wilder side to this road*

best not talked about. It disappears
under scrutiny. You can catch it in glimpses
only after dusk. Seers walk there.

Father staggered into the apartment, his shirt torn, blood running down the side of his face. Mother rushed over to him.

"They called me a Nazi," he gasped. "I was buying a paper on Main Street. I gave the vendor an extra tip because he looked poor. The vendor wouldn't take it from me because of my accent. Some other men came over. They started in on me." He shook his head. "Attacked in Germany for being Jews. Attacked in America for being Germans."

I snuck off into my room. I couldn't bear to look at him. Father always appeared calm and in control, but at that moment, despite his height, he looked small and scared. And that made me feel small and scared too.

→ Chapter Four →

"Yesterday, December 7, 1941—a date which will live in infamy—the United States of America was suddenly and deliberately attacked by naval and air forces of the Empire of Japan."

We sat crowded around the radio. There had been a surprise attack on Pearl Harbor, in Hawaii. I felt so badly for all those soldiers and their families, but I had to admit that a small part of me was glad. I couldn't help it—because this meant America would go to war against Germany and Japan and maybe defeat Hitler before he had a chance to hurt my family and friends who were still in Germany.

We had an assembly the next morning. Mr. Blake, our principal, talked to us about tolerance. He cautioned us not to hate each other because of the color of our skin and reminded us that Japanese-Americans are Americans first and that we live in a democracy. And then he said that German and

Italian students were also good Americans and that we should all remember that. I think my face must have been the color of a red apple. I felt like everyone was staring at me. But at the same time, I was glad that he was taking the time to remind all the students that we were equal, and I was very thankful for that because I'd seen the opposite happen in Germany. When all the terrible things were being said about the Jews there, no one at my school stood up and said it was wrong. In fact, all the teachers and the principal made us feel like the lowest of the low, sometimes even calling us vermin.

Mrs. Ogawa was always happy to have me over for dinner, but the day after Pearl Harbor was attacked, it felt wrong being there. The family was obviously upset. Mrs. Ogawa had tears in her eyes. No one spoke. But the silence wasn't the usual comfortable one that was common in the house; I could feel the anxiety in the air.

"You don't have to leave," John said when I got up to go home for dinner.

"I know," I replied, "but I'd better get going."

As I walked out the door, I could hear his mother start to cry. John walked with me for a bit.

"Father fears for our safety," he explained. "Because we're Japanese."

"But you were born here!" I objected.

"I know. My father worries too much," John scoffed. "I'm an American!"

"Of course you are," I agreed. "This isn't Germany! You aren't going to be singled out. And don't worry," I assured him, "if anyone gives you trouble, I promise I'll take care of them."

"You don't need to say that," John said.

"I know," I replied. "But sometimes we Jews get treated badly because people don't realize we hate Hitler more than they do; they just hear our accent or hear us speak German and hold it against us. And now that might happen to you."

"It won't," he said confidently. "People know us. And I don't mean just me and my family, but, you know, all the Japanese who have lived here a long time. I don't have an accent," he added. Then he realized that might have come out all wrong and he said, "Oh, I'm sorry. You hardly do either, and even if you did, it shouldn't matter."

"But it does matter," I said. "Anyway, don't worry, we'll stick together."

"And remember," John said, "tomorrow I'm going to teach you how to read a box score."

I said good-bye.

On the way home I almost ran right into a mob of boys and men who were breaking windows in the street. My heart leapt into my throat. I hid in a doorway, and then I couldn't help myself; I started to cry. For a while I was paralyzed, unable to move because of the pure terror I felt. But when a few of them found me in the doorway and started to threaten me, I had to run, and I did. The farther I went, the more people I saw—there must have been thousands out on the streets. I overheard them calling to each other and figured out that they were smashing up any home that had a light on because the city was supposed to be in blackout. I knew it wasn't the same, but it seemed like *Kristalnacht* in Berlin all over again.

I hid in doorways, ran when the coast was clear and finally reached our apartment.

"Ben!" Mother exclaimed as I staggered in. She grabbed me and hugged me. "I've been worried sick. Mobs outside and you not home. What were you thinking?"

"Do you think we should go into hiding?" I said, still out of breath.

Mother looked at me with pity, as if I were sick.

"Should we hide?" I repeated.

"They aren't coming after Jews," Father said gently, as if talking to a young child.

"But John says the Japanese are now called Enemy Aliens too," I blurted out. "Just like us. Because we're Germans."

"Yes, because we're *Germans*," Father said. "Not because we're *Jewish*."

"But we're still in danger."

"Not if we don't break any laws," Mother said. Marta took her nose out of her book and glared at me. "You're stupid," she snapped. "We're Americans now. Americans have rights!"

"We had rights in Germany too," I reminded her. "It's easy to take them away—just pass a law. And then get your lawyers to say the new law you passed is legal, that you're doing it for our own good, that we're in danger, that we need to do all these things to protect us against the enemy. They passed laws," I repeated, "and made everything that used to be illegal, legal."

"Just pass a law," she mimicked me. "You're an idiot."

"No, I'm not the idiot! We need at least to think about this, don't we? We waited too long in Germany." I looked at Father then. "But we shouldn't wait too long again."

I ran into my room, shut the door and curled up on my bed. I was shaking and couldn't stop. Everything was repeating itself! It couldn't be happening. We were supposed to be safe here. It wasn't fair! Why couldn't we be safe anywhere? Why?

And then I thought about the promise I'd just made to John. He *was* going to be singled out and I'd promised to stick by him. I couldn't break my promise, but what would it cost me?

Chapter Five

It was only the next morning when I awoke to that awful sound—someone pounding on our door. They were here. I knew it. I had tried to tell Father. But he wouldn't listen. And now it would be too late. They'd take us all away...

"Mr. Friedman?" A voice resonated through the flat.

"Which one?" I could hear Father say. "I am Joseph Friedman. My brother is Isaac."

"It's Isaac Friedman we're looking for. We have a warrant for his arrest."

I heard rustling and doors slamming. I peeked out of the tiny room I shared with Marta. There were two policemen in the hall. Uncle Isaac was putting on his hat. He turned and saw me. He winked. Then he was gone. I threw on my clothes and ran out after him. Mother called after me to stay inside, but I ignored her. I remembered his words to me soon after we'd arrived. "Don't ever be a mug," he'd said to me. "Your father plays by the rules. Won't get him anywhere in this world. Stick with me, kid."

I ran to the police station and arrived covered in sweat and puffing so hard I could barely speak. Once I knew for sure that he was at the station, I raced home to get Father. We both went back down there, but it was hours until we were finally allowed to see Uncle Isaac.

"Ben," he said to me, "you know my associates." He passed me a small piece of paper. "You can find them at this address. They'll make my bail."

"Don't worry, Uncle Isaac," I said. "I'll do it right away."

"Don't give me that look," he said to Father. Father just shook his head and said nothing.

Uncle Isaac's associates told me not to worry, they'd take care of it. One of them, the one I couldn't understand, gave me a dollar. And sure enough, Uncle Isaac came home that night, long after I was supposed to be asleep.

I started to think about what would happen if I needed to fight or even run. I was just a big blob. I decided that after school I was going to run on the track, and I was going to run every day from then on.

Two days later, John missed school. The next day at lunch, I asked him why he'd been away.

"They arrested Father. His business is

importing and exporting Japanese goods, so they say he might be a spy! We're worried. What does it all mean?"

I'd been trying to remain optimistic. I'd been telling myself that Mother was right and I'd been letting my imagination run away with me. But when John told me about his dad something inside me snapped, and the fear I'd managed to squeeze into a small kernel grew in my stomach until it felt like my whole stomach would burst. I felt nauseated. I put down the sandwich I'd been eating. I grabbed John's wrist.

"Whatever happens, if they want to send you away, don't go!" I whispered. "Run away. Maybe they'll send you to a camp. No one gets out of those camps alive."

"This isn't Nazi Germany," John objected, twisting his wrist out of my grasp and giving me a strange look. "They aren't going to kill us." He looked around nervously to see if anyone had overheard me, but we were all alone at our table— a fact that should have told him something. When we first made friends there were always others sitting with us.

"That's what we Jews said," I replied. "We said, 'This is Germany! This is a civilized country. With laws.' But no one ever comes back from those camps. Except as ashes. In urns. It doesn't happen right away. It never does. I know all about that. First, you can't vote. Then you aren't citizens. Then you have to carry special ID cards. Then you're expelled from school. Then you have a curfew and can only sneak out at certain hours as if you are criminals."

"This is different," John insisted.

"Then they arrest innocent people and say they are spies; that's so the population will be afraid. Fear is the government's friend because the more afraid people are, the more you can make them listen to you. They get everyone to spy on everyone else. The Nazis burned the *Reichstag* and blamed it on their political opponents and got into power that way. They made ordinary Germans afraid—afraid of everything and everyone, including other countries. They used us Jews as scapegoats and said the economic problems were all because of us, because Jews controlled the banks. And the thing is, no one said, 'That's just silly, they are our friends and our neighbors.' No, everyone believed the Nazis. And isn't that what's happening with the Japanese here? And if it's happening to you, why not us next? They take away your rights in tiny little slices and you don't even feel it—well, you feel a small nick, and it doesn't hurt that much, but they keep slicing and slicing and suddenly there's no freedom left, there's just bullies left, bullies."

"Ben," John said, his voice low, "even if you are right, what on earth could I do about it? You're making me nervous." He stopped talking and I felt just awful. He was right. What good would it do him at this point, even if all my worst fears came true? Would he run off and leave his mother? Never.

"I'm sorry," I said, suddenly embarrassed by my outburst. "It brings back bad memories, that's all," I added.

"I know," he said. "But I'm not giving up. Nothing bad will happen to us."

I hoped desperately that he was right.

"I'm going to Canada, Ben," Uncle Isaac told me. "Don't want the police breathing down my neck. The only reason I'm out of jail is because I'm an American. But I won't get a fair trial."

"Can I come with you, Uncle Isaac?" I pleaded.

"Sorry, kid. Your dad would never forgive me."

"But he won't listen to me. What if it's *us* who get rounded up next? We have to escape! And anyway, he won't fight if it happens."

"Who's he gonna fight, kid?"

He wrote down the address where he was going. "If you do need to get away, you can all come to Canada, you hear?"

"They won't let John's father out," I said to him. "And he's not even getting a trial."

"That's because he's probably not an American," Uncle Isaac said. "Wouldn't say there's much hope for him."

« »

"Spy! Traitor! Enemy!" Four tenth-graders were shouting as they beat up John in the schoolyard. I raced over and took them all on at once. So they started in on me. "Nazi! Jew!" They got a few good licks in. But the running I'd started doing on the track at lunchtime and after school was starting to pay off. I was getting faster, as well as stronger; not by much, but every little bit helped. I guess they weren't interested in getting hurt, so finally they gave up. I figured I'd have to keep closer tabs on John and try not to let him out of my sight.

It occurred to me that John might not like me hanging around him because it made him stick out more, but I figured it worked both ways. He never asked me to get lost, but if I ever thought he'd be better off without me, well, I'd make myself scarce. But the truth is, the only thing that stops a bully is the chance they might get hurt themselves. They're such cowards! Would those Brownshirts have beat up Jews if the Jews had fought back? But the Jews were too civilized. They weren't organized. They should have fought from the beginning. Instead it was, "Oh, this is Germany. Our country. The model of civilization. Everyone will come to their senses. It can't last. It can't last. It can't last."

What lasts longer than death, I'd like to know?

The morning paper reported that a Chinese man had been found with his head almost cut off. The paper said that he was probably mistaken for a Japanese man.

At school, John looked terrible, like he hadn't slept.

"They've sent my father away," he said so only I could hear. "To a camp called Fort Missoula in Montana."

I didn't know what to say. That I wasn't surprised? And yet part of me was—the part of me that had thought it really *wouldn't* happen here. And if they'd sent his father away, probably John and the rest of his family would be next, and then they'd go after the Germans. Us.

We were standing in line. It was raining. We'd been ordered to turn in our radios and cameras because we were German. Japanese and Italians had to do it too. But apparently we were allowed to keep our guns, if we had any. That was so odd it was almost funny.

"Maybe they're afraid we'll kill people by knocking them on the head with our radios! Or conking them with our cameras," I said.

"You can see their point of view," Father said. "If we were spies, we'd need the radio to get our coded messages. We could take pictures of troops at the docks with our cameras."

I didn't answer. Let him make excuses for them.

"Don't you think we need to get away?" I asked him again.

"Where?" he sighed. "Back to Europe? Where can we go?"

"Canada," I said, remembering Uncle Isaac's words.

"Canada won't be any safer," he said. "It's not the same as before, Ben," he added. "Hitler isn't in power here. They're *fighting* Hitler now. This is the best place to be."

Chapter Six

By the time spring arrived, Enemy Aliens were not allowed to go out between 9:00 PM and 6:00 AM and could only travel to work and school and home again. Was the curfew the first step before a roundup of all Enemy Aliens?

If you opened the newspaper it was Japs this, Japs that. The government used the papers to get everyone to hate the Japanese, just the way they did with the Jews in Germany. Propaganda. It seemed just the same as what happened in Germany, but why was I the only one who could see it? Sure, it wasn't aimed at Jews—*yet*. But in Germany it started with the Jews and no one cared, and soon it was others: gypsies and Communists and anyone else the Nazis hated. Soon it would be Jews in the United States, because Jews are always the scapegoats. Always.

"My older cousin," John whispered, because class had already started, "was so scared about breaking the curfew last night, she didn't go to the hospital when her labor started. Her baby died."

After school, John and I played chess at his house. The only sounds were the rain on the roof and our chess pieces moving on the board.

I didn't bother keeping the curfew. No one stopped me, because I looked like everyone else. John didn't.

Out of nowhere Mother said, "I'd like you to read from the Torah. Be a Bar Mitzvah. You couldn't do it when you should have, on your thirteenth birthday, but there's nothing stopping you now. Don't you want to?"

"Tell everyone I'm a Jew? Of course I do, Mother."

"They already know," she said. She was almost smiling, like it was a joke!

"Well, we don't need to advertise, do we? Here's a Jew to kick!"

"Benjamin!"

"No!"

She shook her head and turned away with that worried look she has half the time when she talks to me.

I knew what was important, though. I didn't have time to study a reading from the Torah! I was already trying to use more American words and phrases, but I needed to practice my English even more so I could get rid of my accent. I had to do well in school. I had to fit in. That way, if I needed to run away, no one would know that I was a Jew. And if the rest of the family refused to see sense and leave, then I'd have to go without them.

"We got a notice this morning in the mail," John told me as we were waiting for class to start. "We have to pack up. We have to get ready to move to a camp." He didn't even say, "I'm an American." He just looked ashamed. I felt myself go cold all over. It was what I'd feared. The worst possible thing. And he was my only friend. What would I do when he was gone? The strange thing was, he was trying to make me feel better. "The Japanese attacked Pearl Harbor," he said, "but just because Americans don't trust us right now doesn't mean they're going to kill us."

"Don't go," I said, but I knew he would.

"I can't leave my family. And where could we hide? It's not as if we can fit in like you. I'd be spotted anywhere I went. It'll be okay. They've told us they'll still have schools for us. The family can stay together. You must calm down."

"I can't calm down! Why does everyone keep telling me that?"

"Because President Roosevelt isn't like Hitler!" he said. "Do you think anyone will harm us? That would be murder!"

What he said sounded logical. But what if there *was* no logic? What then? Sure, you wouldn't get hurt if you weren't Japanese, German or Italian. But he *was* Japanese. And I *was* German. Was anyone going to care that I was a German Jew? They hated Jews in the United States too. Oh yes, I saw that all the time. If they didn't, they would have made it easy for us to come to America. No one else we knew at home made it. We only did because Uncle Isaac is an American and Father had friends who got us visas. But mostly Jews weren't wanted anywhere, were they?

Jews couldn't leave Germany now, but a few years earlier Hitler would've let us all go. No country wanted all those Jews. There was even a headline in a paper at home: *Jews for Sale...Who Wants Them?*

So maybe it wasn't logical. Maybe there was a different rule for Jews and Japanese and Germans—even if you were American or wanted to be.

"The United States is different. It's a democracy," John stated.

"So was Germany," I told him, but my heart wasn't in it. I said it over and over, but no one really seemed to understand. How could they forget that Germany was a democracy before Hitler and his goons got elected? It could happen anywhere. Even in America.

When I got home, Mother took me to see a

doctor. I insisted I wasn't sick, but he examined me and declared that I was suffering from nerves. He asked me if I missed my friends in Germany. And that made me think about Elizabeth.

The Jewish papers blared that Jews were being murdered, gunned down and then thrown into mass graves all over Europe. Did Dr. Meltzer think I didn't read what was in the papers? A priest from Bavaria said the Nazis were experimenting with poison gas as a quicker way to kill Jews in a concentration camp in Austria. Why hadn't I heard a peep from Elizabeth or from Oma and Opa? Mother said it was simply because they were in countries we were at war with and no mail was being allowed through. Maybe. I hoped so.

"Ben," the doctor said, "just go to school and make friends and be a kid. Have some fun. Have you been to the movies? You can't solve the problems of the world by worrying about them. Leave the worrying to the grown-ups."

I stared at him. "Do you think they've done a good job so far?" I asked.

He paused and looked at me for a moment before he replied. "Not particularly," he admitted. "But that doesn't mean there is anything you can do."

I can make plans, I thought. I can think about what needs to be done. And I will.

« »

The day arrived when John's family was to be sent away. I went over to his house.

"Did you see the papers today?" John asked as we walked to his room.

I shook my head. I couldn't stand reading the papers anymore.

"The box scores," he chided me. "The Dodgers won!"

"Really? Thought they'd go into a slump any day." I didn't know much about baseball, but I'd heard John say something like that.

"No! Not with Billie Herman and Pee Wee Reese playing."

He closed his suitcase. "Mother felt much better when you said you would look after the house," he said.

"I'm happy to do it," I assured him.

"We'd better get going," he said. He extended his hand. We shook. I followed him out of his room into the living room. His mother and two older brothers were waiting. Mrs. Ogawa bowed to me. "Thank you for looking after the house, Ben," she said as she handed me the key.

"You're welcome," I said, but it was hard to speak. I felt all choked up. I wanted to yell, "Run! Run! Don't let them take you!" But it was useless. No one listened, no one believed. Everyone was so trusting. Why was that?

All the Japanese were lining up on the street. I was about to go home, but it occurred to me—

why be a patsy? Why sit there and wait for them to come and take me away with the others? John's house was empty so why not just stay there, at least until I saw which way the wind was blowing?

Chapter Seven

I was hungry. I'd been away from home all night, hiding in John's house. I'm sure it wasn't quite what Mrs. Ogawa expected when she asked me to look after the house.

At first it seemed logical. But then I started to worry that it was me that was crazy, not everyone else. *Could* the whole world go crazy, after all? Maybe it could and I was the only sane person left.

I thought about my family, of course, how they wouldn't be able to go to the police because they would be afraid to and how worried they'd be, but somehow I still couldn't bring myself to leave. I drank water from the neighbor's hose.

I decided it was time to sneak back to our apartment, watch and wait until everyone was gone and grab some food. I saw Mother as she hurried out the side door. It looked like she'd been crying. Should I go back to them? They were still there, which meant that the Jews weren't being rounded up yet. Mother walked down the street toward the market.

I went up the stairs two at a time. The Bible on the table was open to the book of Job. I glanced at the passage where Job says, "Who can say to Him, 'What are you doing?'"

I supposed that meant, who are the privileged who get to question God? And even if you did get to talk to Him, would He listen? I read a little farther. "The earth is handed over to the wicked one…. If it's not He, then who?"

"Yeah, if God isn't to blame, who is?"

"Man is."

Father stood at the door.

"You were talking out loud," he explained.

Was I? I stared at him but I didn't answer him. If I started talking I'd end up staying. And I was pretty sure that wasn't a safe thing to do. But not totally sure anymore.

"Where have you been, Ben?" Father didn't budge from the doorway, as if making one move might make me run. "Ben, I know you think you are being sensible. But you're ill. You need to be home with us. You need to trust me. Have I ever let you down?"

What did he mean? Of course he had. Why didn't he get us out of Germany earlier? Why did we have to leave Opa and Oma behind?

"Haven't I kept the family together?" he continued. "Aren't you safe? Ben, talk to me."

Why should I talk to him? He didn't hear me. Just like God wouldn't hear Job. No one listened.

"Ben, you can't just run away. We need you here. What if something does happen? Won't you want to be here? To help protect Mother and Marta?"

Was he saying that just to get me to stay? I wasn't sure. I didn't know what to do.

"Have you eaten?" he asked.

I shook my head but still didn't speak.

"Just sit and eat something."

I was starving. What harm would there be in eating? John's place wasn't going anywhere. I could always go back there—in a few minutes or a few days.

Father moved over to the counter. He started cutting a thick slice of bread. He took a piece of chicken out of the icebox and put it on the board; then he poured me a glass of milk and put it on the table. He motioned for me to wash up.

I washed my hands in the sink and splashed water on my face. I sat down and devoured the food so fast it was gone in a second. Father cut me more bread and spread it with butter. He sliced an apple.

"Mother will be back from the market soon. Eat this for now."

I gulped the milk down.

"Ben, imagine if we suddenly disappeared.

You'd worry, wouldn't you? What you did was cruel."

"I was going to leave a note," I said, breaking my silence.

"Still, gone all night. Where have you been?"

"Somewhere safe."

"There is nowhere safer than with your family. Please, Ben. Don't ever do this again. You need to be in school. You need to be here with us."

"Ben!" Mother was back. She threw her arms around me. "Ben, I've been worried sick. Are you all right?"

I nodded.

"Where have you been?" Now she gripped my shoulders. "Where have you been?"

"I've been fine," I said. "Fine."

"No, I can see you haven't eaten. You haven't washed. Did someone hurt you?"

"I said I'm fine. Why don't you listen to me? We should all be in hiding."

She shook her head in frustration. "We went to the police, but they said they wait at least three or four days to see if you're just a runaway."

They were so worried they even went to the police. I did feel badly then, when I heard that. Maybe I *was* the crazy one.

"I've left the store unattended," Father said. "I need to go down there." He looked at me. "Will you be here when I get back?"

I nodded.

"Go have a bath," Mother said with a sigh.

When I came out of the bathroom Dr. Meltzer was waiting for me.

"I hear you gave your parents quite a scare," he said.

I shrugged. Compared to what? I thought. Hitler?

"Let me have a look at you."

He turned to Mother after he checked me over. "I think he needs something for his nerves."

"No pills," I said.

"You need something to calm you down," he insisted.

"I'm calm. I'm fine."

He wrote out a prescription anyway. "You get this filled," he said to Mother. "Try to get him to take it. He needs to. And maybe a consultation with a psychiatrist."

Mother thanked him and saw him out.

"I'm not crazy!" I said.

"No one said you were crazy," she said. "It reminds me of that joke. Mrs. Levin takes her son to the beach. As soon as they are settled she starts up. 'Adam, be careful, don't go near the water, you'll drown! Adam, don't play like that with the sand. Watch your eyes. You'll go blind. Adam, don't sit in the sun so long, you'll get sunstroke. Oy! Such a nervous child you are!'" She paused. "Come on. Just a little smile."

I tried.

"Even if it's just us being nervous about you, so what can it hurt?"

"Maybe he'll think I'm nuts and put me away. That's what. I'm not talking to a psychiatrist."

"All right. All right. Can you tell me where you've been?"

"No."

"Why? Are you planning to go back? Just disappear again? I'll go crazy if you keep that up. Promise me, Ben. I won't ask you anything else if you promise me not to do it again." When I didn't answer, she said, "It occurred to me this morning—your friend, John, his family was sent away. Was that where you were?"

I guess something in my face gave it away.

"I should have thought of it last night," she said. "I was so panic-stricken I wasn't thinking straight."

My mind was going a mile a minute. Okay. What if I did need to run away? I'd need money. Hiding at John's wouldn't work again. First thing, then, was to get a job.

"Do you think I could sell papers?" I asked.

Mother's expression brightened. "That would be a good idea. An after-school job."

She thought that meant I wouldn't run off. I was sorry I had worried her and Father, but in a way, if it came to another roundup, they'd be glad that I had been smart enough to think ahead, smart enough to escape.

❖ Chapter Eight ❖

My first day back at school, the same four tenth-grade goons who had ganged up on John surrounded me in the schoolyard.

"Where's your little Jap friend? Oh, sent away? Too bad. Next it'll be you Germans. And the Jews! The dirty Jews!"

I was about to throw a punch at the biggest one, but just then Mr. Leahy rushed over. "Break it up! Break it up," he ordered. The four of them glared at me and moved off. I started to walk away when Mr. Leahy took me aside.

"Ben, I've seen you running on the track."

Now what? Was I going to get in trouble for that?

"You're getting to be pretty fast," he commented.

I stared at him. What was this about?

"I'd like you to consider joining the track team."

"Me?" I blurted out, really surprised.

"Yes. We train every day at lunch and some-times after school. You have talent, but you could use some real training if you want to be fast. With your long legs, you could be a great addition to the school team. We have meets and competitions with other schools in the late spring and early summer."

I didn't answer, I was so taken aback.

"Think about it."

Just after lunch, Mr. Bently stopped me in the hallway.

"I understand you and John played chess," he said.

"Yes." Was he going to say something bad about John? I didn't care if he was a teacher, I'd fight him too.

"We've started a chess club this year. We meet after school once a week. Maybe you'd like to join?"

Why were they being nice to me all of a sudden? Maybe Mother had been to the school. That would be just like her, although she was very shy because of her poor English. She could have sent Father. If that was the case, maybe I should agree. If they saw I was participating in school events, they could hardly send me to a psychiatrist who might put me away in some loony bin. "Maybe," I said. "I'll think about it."

I thought it might be good to be on the track team. I'd train better, harder. I'd be in better shape for running away. And I'd look really normal if I joined the chess club.

As soon as school was over, I went down to the newspaper office. They said I could work the corner near our store every morning before school. I was all set. Next time, if I had to run away, it would be for good. No one would find me.

Father brought the book of Job out after supper, and I agreed to work on it with him.

Job is furious with his friends. He says they're taking God's part blindly and stupidly and if they think they're going to be rewarded, they're wrong.

Even those who try to make friends with God and defend Him don't get any special treatment; that's what Job is saying. He's saying they should *wake up*. He's saying God will be as cruel to them as He is to Job, who insists on arguing with God.

"That's the Jewish way," Father said. "That's the key. We argue with God. It's our right."

"We may argue," I grimaced, "but where does it get us? Even Job says there's no point. God will crush you anyway. 'You destroy man's hope.' That's what Job says. Why bother with a God like that?"

"Do we have a choice?" Father said. "I don't think we do."

"Glad to see you'll be joining us, Ben," Mr. Leahy said when I walked onto the track. "Boys, gather

round. Ben, this is, Martin, Craig…" He pointed
to six others, but I didn't catch all their names.
We shook hands; they seemed okay with having
me there.

"Let's get at it," Mr. Leahy said. Then his
manner changed and he became pretty tough.
"Laps, then push-ups," he ordered. I was pouring
sweat by the time we finished. I managed to keep
up with the others, though, which surprised
me—and that's with no formal training. I figured
I might end up being pretty good at it.

At the end of the day, I searched out the chess
club. I stood by the door, looking into the room.
There were about twelve kids, deep into the game.
The room was absolutely quiet.

"You can play your first game against Bill,"
Mr. Bently said as he came over to me, pointing
to a fellow sitting at one of the desks. "His usual
partner has changed schools. That's why we
needed an extra player."

"So," Bill said when I sat down, "I didn't know
Germans could play. I thought they were all busy
ruling the world."

I didn't answer. But my stomach got that
familiar sinking feeling.

"Oh yeah," he added softly. "But you aren't
just a German, are you? Jew too, right? Christ-
killers, last I heard."

"You want to take this outside?" I said.

He was big. A tenth-grader probably, with

blond hair and blue eyes—Hitler's perfect specimen.

"I'd love to," he said, "but first I'll teach you not to play chess with me."

I put up a bit of a fight, but he beat me pretty quickly. I thought about quitting, but it would be better revenge to get so good I could beat him. He'd never believe a Jew could be smart enough.

On my way home from school, Bill and two of his friends, just as big as he was, stopped me. They could kill me if they tried, but I didn't care. Bill was too chicken to fight by himself; I could see that.

"Need some help?" I taunted him. "Can't fight me alone?"

I was on the ground before I knew it, sucker-punched in the jaw. I struggled to get up.

"I don't need any help," he said as he walked away.

Mother fussed over me something terrible when I got home. "Who did this? I'll go to the principal! To the police!"

"No! I can take care of myself."

"Sure looks like it," Marta said. They were almost the first words she'd spoken to me since I'd returned from John's house. Just before I went to sleep the night I came back, she had whispered, "You *are* crazy, Ben. We're okay here. It's you that's not okay. *You*." She was so mad at me for worrying everyone she wouldn't speak to me after that.

Didn't she remember the roundups in Berlin? Didn't she remember *anything*? Didn't she hear them calling us dirty Jews?

But she was just a kid. I couldn't blame her. I could only blame Father.

❖ Chapter Nine ❖

I played Bill again on our second meeting, and he beat me again, but it wasn't quite so easy for him. My plan was simple: first, beat him at chess and then beat him up. He had a problem with me being a Jew? Just wait. I'd give him a problem.

When I got home there was a letter sitting on the kitchen table. "That's for you," Mother said. My heart leapt in my chest. Elizabeth? I scooped it up, looking at the name and return address. John. I sat at the table.

> *Dear Ben,*
> *We're in a town called Puyallup. It's only twenty-five miles away from Seattle, so you might have heard of it. We have been put in the Assembly Center. It's where they hold their state fair. They call this place Camp Harmony. No one here thinks the name is funny. It is surrounded by barbed wire. Soldiers patrol the fences. We are prisoners. I begin to worry that*

*you were right all along. Perhaps we really
are in danger from our own government.*

*We are living in shacks. The ground is just
covered with boards, and grass grows between
the cracks. We had to stuff straw into sacks
for mattresses. There is mud everywhere.
The toilet is a board with holes cut in it.*

*Every morning they check us with a roll
call. They barge into our rooms whenever
they want and search our things. They took
away all our Japanese books.*

*The adults are trying to make it seem
normal. They've put street signs up, elected
a mayor, and they call the mess halls names
like Jackson Cafe or Spice's Cafe, but they're
still mess halls. The food is not bad, though,
because it's all cooked by chefs who had their
own restaurants. There are even special
meals for kids. We had a dance on Saturday.
We tuned all our radios to the same station
and everybody danced. Pretending it was just
a regular Saturday night. But it wasn't, was
it?*

*I am an American. Why is this
happening?*

*We do get the papers, so I've decided that
since it's spring I'm going to start to follow
baseball more closely as a hobby. My brother
Michael suggested it. He says he'll play chess
with me too. He says we have to make the best*

*of it, there's no point in getting blue. He is the
head of the family now, so I will try to listen
to him.*

Hope you and your family are well.
John.

I wondered if I should go there and try to help
him escape. But what was the point? He wouldn't
come with me; he wanted to be with his family.

A lot of the boys working at the paper were
using their money to buy war bonds, but not me.
My plan to run away was gaining steam. After that
letter, it seemed like the only sane thing to do. I
decided that I'd save every penny so eventually I
could go to Canada and live with Uncle Isaac. He
knew what was what. I'd stick with him.

The next time I sat down across from Bill to play
him, he said to me, "I'll tell you what. You pay
me a buck and I won't beat you up after school.
Jews always have lots of money. That shouldn't be
a problem."

"I'll tell *you* what," I said. "You pay *me* a buck
and I won't beat you at chess right now."

He threw his head back and laughed. "Hey,
don't make me laugh too hard," he said. "I won't
be able to think straight."

I tried to remember everything I'd learned
about chess. I concentrated so hard I felt like I'd
burst, but in the end he still beat me.

"Checkmate," he said, the biggest grin in the world on his face. "See you later."

I took a deep breath and started the walk home. Sure, I could have run. He'd never catch me. But I was no chicken. I could take whatever he gave me. After all, I'd been beaten up by a whole gang of Hitler Youth. One day after school in Berlin, me and my friend Josh walked right into them; we turned a corner and there they were. Josh was dark and small. They guessed we were Jews right away. First they pushed us around for a while just to get us scared. Then they started punching. Once we were on the ground they started kicking. I was lucky. After just a week in bed I could walk again, but Josh had internal bleeding and almost died. He never really got better. Yeah, Bill and his friends didn't scare me.

I walked a few blocks before Bill and his two pals found me.

"Give up," Bill said. "Drop the chess club. I'll leave you alone. If those morons on the track team don't care about running with you, that's their problem, but I don't want you stinking up the chess club." I stared at him, stood my ground and didn't grace him with an answer. "I'm talking to you!" he shouted.

I spat on the ground, right in front of him.

"Why—you!" He lunged at me. He was so mad he lost his balance. I swung my books upward, right into his nose.

Whack. What a great sound. He reeled back, blood spurting from his schnoz.

"You rotten kike," he shouted. "Get him!" he yelled at his friends.

One of them held me. The other hit me hard in my stomach. Bill came in with a punch to the face. His friends let go and I staggered, desperately trying to stay on my feet.

"Got something to say now?"

"Yeah," I grunted, "you'd be a great Nazi. Why don't you go sign up?"

He hit me again, this time on the jaw, and I went down. The cold sidewalk felt good on my face. My head was spinning.

They left me there. I got back home after a while, making sure Mother didn't see me before I'd cleaned up. Even so, when she came into my room to say hello, she could tell right away—my jaw had turned black-and-blue within minutes.

"Ben, tell me who's doing this or I'm going to the principal."

"I can take care of it!"

"No, you can't!"

"If I don't stand up for myself it'll just get worse," I insisted. "Leave it." She got me a piece of ice and made me hold it against my jaw.

Later I could hear her talking about it with Father.

"Let the boy make his own decisions," he said. "He has to be at school, not you."

"They'll kill him!"

"He knows all about survival," Father said. "No one's going to kill him."

Was that a compliment from Father? Did he think it was a good thing that I knew how to survive? I couldn't tell from his voice.

Then Mother said, "I won't let it go on indefinitely. I won't. We have to protect him."

I almost dashed out of my room and screamed at them, "Why don't you, then? Why don't you *really* protect me? Why don't you get me out of here?"

✦ Chapter Ten ✦

I was still sore from Bill's beating when the four gorillas who had tormented John met up with me just before track.

"You still here?" one of them said. He had a front tooth missing and his hair was cut so short you could see his scalp. His shirt was almost split at the bottom because of his huge belly. He was the leader. I didn't even know his name. The other three were definitely under his control and probably pretty harmless on their own.

I stood there and waited. I'd fought them before and I'd do it again.

"Why didn't you go away with your friend John? Can't see why they don't lock the Germans up with the Japs."

"Hey, Ben," a voice called. "Coming to track?"

I glanced over. Martin Mitchell, from the track team, was standing there, along with Steven and Craig.

"I have some business here first," I called to them.

Martin pushed his way past the goons and stood beside me.

"Oh yeah? If they've got business with you, they've got business with the whole team." He stared at the big guy. "Hey, Lester, you finished here? We've got practice."

Lester started to open his mouth. Then he looked over at Steven and Craig and shrugged. "I'm finished," he said. "Just having a word with the Jew here."

"A word is about all you've got in your vocabulary," Martin said.

"Hey, you insulting me?"

"What do you think?"

Lester wasn't sure, which was pretty funny.

"Well, don't," Lester growled. Then he motioned for his boys and they left.

I wondered for a moment if I should thank Martin—but why should I? I hadn't asked for his help, had I? He didn't have to stick his nose in. I could've handled them myself. I didn't need anyone's help. I said nothing.

"Come on," he said. "We'll be late for practice."

He didn't seem to expect any big thanks, which was a good thing because he wasn't going to get any.

Still, I couldn't say I was sorry I didn't have

to fight again. I was still pretty sore from the day before.

I didn't run as well as I should have that day because my stomach still hurt when I moved. I could still feel that fist. Lester was a pushover compared to Bill.

After practice Martin came over to me. "A bunch of us go over to the ice-cream parlor every Thursday after school, to break training. Want to come today?"

I was so taken aback that for a minute I couldn't answer. He must have thought my silence meant no. "Meet us there if you want. It's on Fourth Street."

I wondered if they were just setting me up so I'd go and no one would be there. Or maybe they planned to fight me. He turned with a shrug and walked off. Could the invitation be legit? I doubted it.

I happened on Mr. Bently in the hall at lunch and he asked me how I liked the chess club.

"I can't beat Bill," I said. "But I'd like to."

"Come to my room after class today," he suggested. "I'll give you a few tips."

I did and he showed me a pretty swell strategy.

"It's not one of the things I usually teach," he said. "Might take your partner by surprise. But do you want me to switch you to another partner?"

Had he heard something?

"No," I answered quickly. Bill might think I was backing down, and that would be no good. I couldn't have that. I never backed down.

Father had just closed up the shop and was busy translating Job when I got home. I had to admit that I was getting a little more interested in the book of Job. Job often seemed to say just what I was thinking. He asked why the wicked live on and prosper while the righteous are punished. Job's friends just didn't get it, though. How did they react when Job said that bad people get rewarded and the good don't? They went on and on about how Job and anyone who had hard luck must be *bad* and that's why they were being punished.

The trouble with those friends of Job was that they had no imagination. None. They assumed that if you were good you'd be rewarded by God; if you were bad you'd be punished. They couldn't accept that God might be doing things all wrong. Shouldn't Elizabeth be living in Seattle, happy and healthy? Shouldn't Bill be tortured by the Nazis?

I wished I could talk to those friends of Job. If you return to God you'll be restored, they said. But Job never left God. God left Job. God betrayed Job. That's what they should call God. The betrayer.

Father disagreed when I told him what I thought. "Only man can betray man," he argued.

"You don't blame God for anything?" I asked.

"Why should I?"

"There's a lot to blame Him for. The Nazis."

"So I should praise Him for good and blame Him for evil?"

"Maybe."

"But if He hadn't created both, what would we be?"

"What do you mean?"

"I mean we wouldn't be human. We'd be puppets who only do good. This world would be nothing at all like it is now."

"But that would be an improvement."

"When something good does happen, isn't there satisfaction if you helped it happen? That you worked for the good? What would be the point if the decisions we made didn't matter? If we couldn't choose between good and evil, what would be the point of being human? Isn't choice the point?"

"It's a stupid point," I objected. "I'd rather be a puppet than have to see all these terrible things. Anyway, He's God. He could have come up with a better system. This one doesn't work. Even if you choose good, like you say, you end up smacked down. What about Elizabeth? What about Oma and Opa?"

Father paused. Quietly he said, "God did not hurt them. The Nazis hurt them. *If* they've been hurt," he added.

"God made the Nazis," I screamed, completely losing my temper.

"No," he said. "God made people. And the German people have chosen Hitler, and the Nazis have chosen to be Nazis."

I threw my pen down and got up from the table. "He'd be better off not making innocent people who are just going to suffer. He makes the rules. Why can't He change them?"

Father stood up too. "Even if what you say is true, and the whole setup stinks—which I don't agree with—it's the way it is. That's the one thing we can't change—the basic rules of existence. But we still have to choose how to live in this world. We still have a choice."

"Choice. Right."

I had lots of choices. What he didn't know was that one of them was not to live with him anymore.

→ Chapter Eleven ←

Chess club finally came around again and I could barely wait to get started. Bill had no idea that I had a new strategy, so I caught him completely unawares with Mr. Bently's surprise attack—and suddenly he was finished!

I stood up.

"That's the last time I'll play you," I said. "I had enough of guys like you in Germany."

"What do you mean by that?"

He stood up too.

Mr. Bently came over. "Any problem here, boys?"

"Nope," I said. "But I'd like a different partner next week."

"Probably a good idea," Mr. Bently agreed.

Bill turned beet red. "I'll see you after school," he said.

Not if I can help it, I thought. I mean, I didn't have to be a patsy for him to pound into hamburger meat, and if he couldn't find me he couldn't beat me up. Now that I'd shown him I could beat him at chess, I didn't need to be his punching bag.

I took a different route and managed to get home without seeing him. I felt pretty good about beating him at chess. I thought I should write to John and tell him all about it, including the strategy Mr. Bently showed me because John might be able to use that on his brother. But I couldn't seem to make myself write him.

In the middle of the night there was a big crash downstairs. Father told us all to stay put, but I followed him anyway.

We saw that the front window had been shattered by a huge rock that was now lying on the floor of the store. Father ran outside. I followed. A banner was hanging from the door. It must have been put there before the rock was thrown, but in the dark of the blacked-out street it was impossible to see what it said. Father tore it down and dragged it inside. He made sure the door was closed and the windows covered before he turned on the light. In large red hand-painted letters were the words *Germans go home.*

"Let's get some wood from the back and burn this up," he said.

He sent me to tell Mother and Marta that everything was all right, but I didn't believe it was. I remembered how on *Kristalnacht* all the Jewish stores had rocks thrown through their windows. I remembered the broken glass, the writing—*Jews Out! Jew!*—scrawled across the shop doors. All the time I was helping Father clean up, I couldn't stop thinking about how to get out of there. It was time—it was past time. I'd been saving money for weeks. I'd catch a bus to the border, and then I'd sneak across and hitch a ride to Vancouver to find Uncle Isaac. He was fast. He was sneaky. He was always one step ahead, and that was the only way to survive.

When I woke up I wondered if I should put it off for a few more weeks or even just a few more days. But our family was a target now. No. It was time.

I pretended to leave for school, but instead I went straight to the bus depot. I had enough money for a ticket to Bellingham. I bought it, and then I went home midmorning, making sure Mother was out at the market before I went into the apartment. I packed some food and some extra clothes in my knapsack and returned to wait at the station. I ate a beef sandwich and treated myself to an ice-cream bar.

My family wouldn't realize I was gone until dinnertime, and by then I'd be across the border.

The bus trip only took an hour. I sat beside an old woman who chattered to me about her grand-children. I tried not to think about my Oma, left behind, probably dead. I nodded politely, and then I pretended to sleep because it hurt too much to listen to her. When I got off the bus I really wasn't sure what to do next. If I asked straight out where the border was, it might sound suspicious. But then I thought, so what? I doubted anyone would care enough to actually *do* anything, so I asked the person behind the ticket counter.

"Why do you want to know?" He was an old guy.

"Schoolwork," I answered quickly. "We're supposed to ask people in authority these questions to see if they are ready for war."

"Oh." And he told me. It wasn't far to the town limits, but then I had to figure out the best thing to do. I saw a dirt road, which I assumed led to Canada. I decided to follow it.

I walked for hours and never saw a soul. After a while I didn't know whether I was still in the United States or not, and it was starting to get dark. I passed some farms, but no one was on the road. I began to suspect that I was lost; unless the road met up with a larger one, I'd have to go back. Finally it was too dark to go on, so I settled down under a tree, putting on my jacket and an extra sweater. It was cold, but at least it wasn't raining. Every once in a while I got up and ran around just to warm up. It was a long night and I couldn't help but think about our cozy apartment and how worried Mother must be. Still, if they'd listened to me, none of this would have been necessary.

As soon as there was just a little bit of light

I started to walk again. And then I heard a car coming up behind me. It slowed when it came alongside, and then it stopped. A man looked out at me from inside an old jalopy.

"Where you off to, son?"

"Vancouver."

"Strange way to get there."

"Why?"

"Because you're going the wrong way. Vancouver's west. You're headed east. I'm going to White Rock. You can get a bus from there. Want a ride?"

"Yes, please."

"Get in then."

I did.

"I'm Dr. Francis," the man said. He was about my dad's age, with glasses and flecks of gray in his black hair. "You been out all night? You all right?"

"I'm fine."

"Your parents know where you are?"

I had to think fast.

"My parents were hurt in a fire. I'm going to my uncle in Vancouver."

"Well, I'm sorry to hear that, but I'm sure the authorities could've sent you. I hate to see you walking like this."

"I want to be with family," I said. "Just want to be there. Going to the authorities would take too long."

He gave me a long look, and then he seemed to accept my story. What worried me was whether or not I was still in the United States because I wouldn't be able to openly cross the border. I decided to keep my mouth shut and hope for the best.

Within half an hour we drove into a town and I spotted the Union Jack flying over the post office. We were in Canada! Dr. Francis dropped me in front of a small café. "Bus stops here at eight o'clock in the morning. Do you have enough money?"

"I have some," I said.

He fished in his pockets; then he passed me two dollars. "Here. You'll need some food. This'll pay for the fare."

"Why are you doing this?" I asked, suspicious.

He grinned. "What's the matter? No one ever done you a favor before?"

I didn't answer.

"We're a small community here," he explained. "We like to help people."

For some reason I could feel tears rise up in my eyes.

"Hey, hey, hey, it's nothing," he assured me.

I couldn't answer him. I felt all choked up. He waved and drove off.

I used a little of the money—ten cents—to buy a piece of pie at the café. Then I waited for the bus. It arrived right on time, and there I was, on my way to Vancouver and Uncle Isaac. He had said I could come, hadn't he? I just hoped he was still there. In a way, I couldn't believe what I'd just done. Run away. For real.

Well, Father couldn't be trusted, could he? A rock through the window and he'd fix the glass, then pretend nothing had happened. But I knew it had happened. What would be next? A firebomb, a bullet, a knife attack? Let him close his eyes, let him pretend everything would be fine. I wasn't so dumb. Not me.

I pushed aside any feelings of guilt about him and especially Mother. And I stopped asking myself if I was going overboard, going crazy. I decided everyone else was.

→ Chapter Twelve ←

Once I reached the bus station in Vancouver, I showed the driver Uncle Isaac's address. He told me what local bus to catch and where to catch it. It was lunchtime and I was hungry, but I wanted to find Uncle Isaac as soon as I could. I had to change buses twice, but finally I got off near his street, which was in a pretty seedy part of town. I walked to the address he had given me. It turned out to be a small hotel called the Sunrise. I went to the front desk and asked for Uncle Isaac. The man behind the desk gave me his room number. I walked down the hall and knocked, but there was no answer. I figured if he had a job it would make sense that he'd be out, so I returned to the small lobby, found a chair, sat down and waited. I waited all afternoon. I was very hungry and thirsty. I decided to spend some money at a coffee shop attached to the hotel. I ordered a glass of milk and a chicken salad sandwich. The waitress added a piece of apple pie. I started to tell her I had no money for it, but she said, "It's okay, kid. You look hungry. And it's the last piece. If you don't complain it ain't fresh enough, I won't tell that I let you have it." She winked at me. Her hair was the color of wheat and she looked pale and tired, but she smiled at me so nicely.

Already I started to feel better. Safer. Everyone in Canada had been so nice to me—a complete stranger. I thanked the waitress, went back to the lobby again and sat in a chair, holding my knapsack on my lap.

Finally, at exactly 5:15 by the huge clock on the wall, Uncle Isaac walked in. He didn't see me at first. He looked tired. I noticed how his hair was getting a little gray. I wondered why I had never noticed that before.

"Uncle Isaac!" I jumped up.

He turned toward me. His face lit up. "Benjamin!" Then he looked worried and hurried over to me. "What's the matter? Has something happened?"

"No. Everyone is fine at home. But they wouldn't listen to me. Someone threw a rock into our window and left a big banner saying *Germans Go Home*. Next it'll be a firebomb. I tried and tried to tell Father we had to leave. But he wouldn't listen."

Uncle Isaac looked puzzled. "So what are you doing here, Ben?"

"I just came by myself."

"And your father let you?"

"Not exactly."

He frowned. "You ran away?"

"I had to!"

"Oy. Ben. What were you thinking? Your parents, they'll be worried sick."

"No, they won't. I ran away last month, and then I went home. They probably know I'm okay."

"We're going straight to the telegraph office to send them a wire," he said. "Come on. We'll put your bag in my room. Guess we'll have to share a bed."

I followed him down the hall to his room, which was just a tiny place with a cupboard and a bed and a small table beside the bed.

"It's not a palace, but I don't need much," he said. "The business, the apartment, everything else is okay?"

"Fine. Business is good, Father says. Seems like practically everyone in town has jobs in the Boeing plant and they all want new furniture."

"Good. Good. I know he'd rather be teaching at the university, but this is fine for now. Maybe one day he can teach German, the way he used to teach English. I don't think at the moment there's much call for that."

"No." I *almost* laugh just because I'm so happy. He'd practically said I could stay and share the room, and now I'd be safe. I felt light as a feather!

"Come on," he said. "First the telegram."

We walked for a few blocks into a nicer part of town. Everything seemed brighter suddenly. I noticed the leaves on the trees, how green it all was, the blue sky, the faint smell of the ocean, the flowers everywhere. I suddenly realized I hadn't even been naming the flowers in my head the way I used to. I'd almost forgotten all about them.

"It's pretty here," I said.

"No prettier than Seattle," he answered.

"Oh, I think it is. What are you doing, Uncle Isaac? Do you have a job?"

"I'm here illegally, so I can't get an official job. That takes papers. But I've got a few things going. You know me, kid. Can't keep me down for long. And your father sends money from the business."

"Will you ever be able to come home?" I asked.

"I'm not sure," he replied. He looked sad. "I'm thinking maybe I should have stayed, faced the music. They didn't really have much on me. Small numbers racket. You know."

"But you're German; they might have punished you just for that."

"Don't forget, Ben, I'm an American."

"Tell me the story again, of how you came to America."

"At dinner. I'll tell you at dinner."

He sent the wire to Father. *Ben safe in Vancouver with me.*

« »

Meat loaf was the dinner special in the hotel coffee shop. It was delicious. While we ate, I begged Uncle Isaac again to tell me the story of how he came to America.

"Your Oma and Opa," he said, "they were very strict. Your father, he didn't mind. He was always a good boy. But me, I was always trouble." I liked this part. "I used to skip school. I hated books. I liked to get into mischief. Opa, he used the strap on me, he punished me. Nothing worked. Finally I decided to ask him to help me get a visa for America. He agreed. I was sixteen. And when my papers came through, I traveled over as a ship's dishwasher. Weeks with my hands in the suds. And that first day we came into port? I was so scared! But I soon started as an apprentice to Mr. Cohen, at the furniture shop. And when he got sick and died, he left me the store because he was a widower with no children of his own. He had become like a father to me. One who never punished me." He paused. "You're lucky with your father," Uncle Isaac added. "Your Opa could be a hard man."

"He never laughed," I agreed. "Not like Oma."

"Neither do you," Uncle Isaac observed.

"I have my reasons," I said, looking down.

"I'm sure he did too."

I looked back up at him. "I'm not like him!"

"It's easy to be like him. It's easy to be hard."

"It's easier to be *soft*," I said.

"Do you like it here?" I asked, to change the subject. "Where do you work?"

"Oh, I get things here and there. But it ain't that easy. Not without papers. Not with my German accent."

"But people are nice here!"

"Yeah, nice if you ain't German or Italian or Japanese."

"But they haven't sent the Japanese away here like at home!"

"What makes you think that?"

I stopped, stupefied.

"Don't you read the papers?" he asked.

"I look at the headlines when I'm selling the papers so I can call out a catchy phrase or something. But I never noticed anything about Vancouver."

"They're all being rounded up here. In fact, there was a riot just the other day—Japanese men being held downtown before being sent away. They threw chunks of plaster, iron gratings, even toilet paper into the streets because they're being sent to these horrible road camps in the interior without their families. At least at home the families are kept together. These men are going into the rough. Their property's been taken away." He shook his head. "Worse than at home."

I stared at him. "It can't be," I exclaimed. "Everyone is so nice here."

"Would I joke about something like that?"
"So it's not safe anywhere?"
"Kid, it never has been."

Chapter Thirteen

I couldn't sleep. I just kept lying there, listening to Uncle Isaac snore and wondering where to go, what to do. After all, if they were arresting the Japanese in Canada, then Jews weren't safe here either. The Jews could be next. How could I have been so stupid? I might as well have stayed and hidden out at the market on the waterfront in Seattle. At least I knew the area a little.

On the other hand, I thought, maybe it would be safe to stay here. No one seemed to notice Uncle Isaac. But he did have a heavy accent. And if I stuck with him and they went after him, they'd come after me next.

I wasn't sure what to do. I needed a new plan. But what?

Someone was knocking on my head. Stop it. Stop it.

"Ben, wake up."

I sat up.

Father was standing over the bed.

"What...?" I figured I must be dreaming.

"Ben," Father said. "Are you awake?"

"I don't know."

"It's one o'clock in the afternoon. Uncle Isaac let you sleep in. I've come to take you home."

"How did you get here?"

"I took a bus to the border, waited until dark and crossed over through a farmer's field. Then I caught a bus at White Rock. Just got here."

Father did all that?

"Cat got your tongue?"

"Get dressed," Uncle Isaac said to me. "We'll go eat something."

I washed up in the bathroom down the hall and got dressed. We went to the café and ordered egg salad sandwiches.

"Here's the thing," Father said, not bothering to lecture me, but getting right to business. "If we are caught on the way back, while still in Canada, we could be deported to Germany or sent to a camp. I've heard that German Jews are being held in a camp in the east—Ontario maybe. I'm not sure exactly what will happen to us if we're caught, but it won't be good. I had a close call on the way here. The borders are being guarded. You see, Ben, we aren't US citizens yet, and we certainly have no Canadian papers. And the US border guards won't let us back in, because we left illegally."

"We'll be killed if we go back to Germany."

"The border guards don't care. We left the country without permission. We can't get back in—not legally anyway. We'll have to sneak back."

"I'm not going back!" I said.

"What's your plan?" Father asked.

"Maybe stay with Uncle Isaac, maybe live rough. It'll be safer than being a target."

"I have to go back, Ben. I have your mother and Marta to look after. What will they do if *I* can't get back?"

"You shouldn't have come. It was stupid."

"Now you watch your lip," Uncle Isaac said. "Your father was brave. He came at risk to his own safety." He looked at me. "I know you don't like to talk about what happened, Ben, but don't you think your father deserves some credit? Getting you out of Germany—it took lots of brains to keep one step ahead of the Nazis. Most didn't get out."

"We waited too long," I said, trying not to yell and attract attention. "We waited way too long."

"Because you shouldn't run unless you have to. You're still running," Father said. "But it's time to stop. It's not the same here as in Germany. The police have been by the store. Officer Mulgrew says he'll keep a special watch out for the hooligans. In Berlin the police *were* the hooligans. It's not the same, Ben."

He could babble all he wanted. It *was* the same. I knew it was. I started wondering when I should go. Right after lunch? Just walk out the door, get a bus, get lost somewhere. That was the only answer. Even if Uncle Isaac was right and Father wasn't a coward, Father was still kidding himself. Officer Mulgrew wouldn't help us, not really, not with our being German. And if they didn't hate us for that, they'd hate us for being Jews. How could Father be so blind?

"I need you to help me get back," Father said to me.

"What?"

"We're going to have to plan how to get back. I need your help, Ben. I can't get caught at the border. Your mother needs me."

"So why did you come?"

He looked at me. "Because you need me too."

"I don't need anyone. You got here alone. I'm sure you can get back alone."

I got up. Although I didn't have my knapsack and wasn't sure how to run away, it seemed to me that the important thing was just to go, get away, right away, right then. So I turned and sprinted out of the café's front door. Father ran after me, calling my name, but once outside there was no way he could catch me. I turned on the speed and ran as fast as I could.

After a while I looked over my shoulder. Father

was nowhere in sight. I still had a bit of money left in my pockets, which I used to get on a bus. I asked the bus driver for directions to the waterfront. Two bus changes later, I finally saw it and got off the bus. It was busy, just like in Seattle. There were warehouses, trucks, a market. I headed over to the market and started asking at each stall if anyone needed help. Soon a big beefy guy said he'd give me fifty cents for an afternoon's work unloading vegetables into trays. I agreed. He didn't ask me any questions about why I was there. He didn't care.

By the end of the afternoon I was beat, but I'd made enough money to buy dinner, plus he let me have two apples and a banana. By then I felt that I was set. I could work there and have enough to eat. I found a small coffee shop and got the special and a Coke for my fifty cents. After dinner I wandered around. I needed somewhere to sleep. Beside a warehouse I found an abandoned truck missing two wheels. I climbed in the back and settled down as well as I could. I was wearing a sweater, but I wasn't sure that would be enough to keep out the cold.

Should I have stayed? Helped Father get back? And maybe get caught along with him? And get sent back to Germany?

Yellow belly a voice inside me said. But I wasn't a coward; I just didn't want to be stupid. I mean, why get caught? But Father had risked being sent back to Germany just to find me. I shook my head. No use thinking about all that. I decided to try to get some sleep.

The next morning I woke up in the truck and over-heard two fellows talking about work to be had over at Hastings Park. I followed them to a nearby bus stop. I had just enough for the bus fare there and back. Soon we were getting off at a street near the water's edge and I followed them into a huge com-plex called the Pacific National Exhibition Grounds. There were large buildings that smelled like they'd been used for animals that came to perform or be exhibited at a fair. Inside there was chaos—people coming and going in no seeming order, and people packed together in the stalls where animals should be. Japanese people. I suddenly felt like I couldn't breathe. I backed away slowly, and then I turned and ran. I ran and ran until I didn't know where I was. I climbed on a bus and asked how to get back to the downtown waterfront.

Once there, I tracked down the fellow who had given me work the day before and made the same deal with him. By night I was exhausted and so miserable I started to think I should go back to the hotel and face the music, whatever it was. But it was dark, and after I ate I had no bus fare, so I figured I'd wait until the morning before I decided what to do. I found the same truck and settled down as best I could.

A very bad decision, as it turned out.

⇸ Chapter Fourteen ⇷

There was something cold on my neck. I opened my eyes, but it was pitch dark.

"Don't move. That's a knife at your throat."

Whoever was speaking had breath that reeked so bad it was hard not to turn away. I felt the cold blade against my skin. It flashed through my mind that I could have been with Father and that maybe I was going to die then and there and no one would ever know. And all because I'd been trying to keep myself safe. I almost laughed but managed not to. It probably would have come out as a squeal anyway, because I was so scared I could hardly breathe.

"Got any money?"

"A little." When I spoke I could feel the blade cut into my skin and then something wet seeped down my neck and onto my shoulder. Blood.

"Where?"

"In my pocket."

"Give it to me."

"If I move, the knife'll cut me more."

"I'm taking it away. Just a bit. Don't try anything funny."

I reached into my pocket, put my hand around the couple of pennies I had left and slowly pulled them out.

"What've you got?"

"Two dollars," I lied. He'd kill me if he knew how little I had. "And more in my back pocket. But I have to get up."

"Okay. You get up slow."

I had to take a chance—this guy would kill me as soon as he saw there was no money. I rested on my toes as I was getting up, got my balance, and then I lunged forward with all my strength, pushing the guy back. He fell over backward, but the knife sliced upward and cut my ear. There was no time to worry about that. I leapt off the truck. It was far too dark to see, but I needed to run and I did. I stumbled. I could hear him swearing as he followed me. I knew I needed to get to a well-lit street so I could put on the speed, so he wouldn't be able to catch me, but just then I crashed over someone sleeping on the ground. I fell.

I smelled liquor, but whoever I'd fallen over was too drunk to care. I scrambled up and kept running. I looked back over my shoulder, and I saw someone in the faint light of a streetlamp. He was big. Huge. I darted behind a building; then I ran toward another one. I found myself on a small street, barreled down it, checked again and saw that he was still behind me. The small street led to a bigger one where there were houses. I needed to make noise.

"Help!" I tried to scream, but I didn't have enough breath. I looked back. He was still there, so I kept running. I looked back again. It seemed that he was starting to drop back. I kept going. I didn't know where or for how long. I kept running. Finally I slipped behind a house in a residential area. I couldn't catch my breath. I was crying. Somehow it felt like *Kristalnacht*, and then I didn't care anymore what happened to me. I was too tired. I didn't want to survive. Or fight. Or live. It was too hard. I could feel the blood oozing from my ear, my neck. I closed my eyes. Sleep. Best to sleep.

"Son. Son. Wake up. Wake up."

A man in white stood over me. "We're going to pick you up now."

I didn't want to wake up. Let them kill me while I slept if they wanted to. I didn't want to wake up. I wanted to sleep forever. Forever.

"Son. Wake up."

Didn't want to. Couldn't make me.

"Son, can you hear me?"

I could sense daylight.

"Son, can you hear me?"

Sleep. Let me sleep.

"Young man." It was a woman's voice. "Young man, please wake up. Right now."

I opened my eyes before I remembered I'd vowed not to. There was an angel dressed in white standing over me. She was all golden: long curly golden locks flowing down her shoulders with a golden light behind her. "That's better," she said with a smile. "What's your name?"

Dead people probably didn't have names. I hoped I didn't have to meet God. Or He better hope He didn't have to meet me. Yeah, He better hope that. Because it wouldn't be nice—not at all. He'd never be able to explain the Nazis to me. Let Him *try* to explain the Nazis.

"Stay alert, young man," the angel ordered me. "I need to know your name." She gave me a sip of water from a straw. I drank. I couldn't be dead. The water felt so good going down my throat. I moved my eyes. There were people all around. White walls. I was in a hospital.

"Doctor, he's awake."

An older man came over.

"Hello, young fellow. We almost lost you," he said. "You bled pretty badly. It looks like you were in a terrible fight. What happened?"

What should I tell him?

"The police were around earlier. They want

to know the details so they can get you back home." I must have looked alarmed because he said, "Don't worry, they aren't blaming you."

They *would* blame me once they knew I wasn't supposed to be in Canada. They'd send me back to Germany or put me in a camp. I had to get back to Father. I had to get out of there.

I tried to smile. "Thanks for helping me," I croaked. "My name is Ben Wilson. I was working late at the docks and missed my bus. I must've fallen asleep in the truck. Then this big guy attacked me. That's all I remember."

"What's your address, Ben? We'll call your family."

Think. Think. Think.

"I'm staying with family friends at the Sunrise Hotel. Call Isaac Friedman there."

He nodded to the nurse to do it.

"Am I hurt badly?"

"No. You've lost a bit of your ear lobe. You were bleeding slowly but steadily from that neck wound. Any longer and you might have died. But we've got you all stitched up now. You lost a lot of blood. You'll need to rest for at least a week. We'll keep you here another day just to be sure you are all right."

I had to get out of there before the police came back. I had to...Suddenly I was so tired I couldn't keep my eyes open.

"You sleep. You'll feel better when you wake up."

I didn't want to sleep anymore, but it seemed I couldn't help it...

"Ben. Ben."

I opened my eyes.

It was Father!

"Ben, listen to me. We have to leave here. I know you're weak. Ben. Wake up. Uncle Isaac is waiting outside in a cab. Ben. Close your eyes. I'm going to take the needle out of your arm."

I closed my eyes. It hurt when he took the needle out.

"Can you sit up?"

I tried. My head started to spin. "Come on. I'll help you. I have a wheelchair."

He lifted me into the chair; I don't know how.

"The nurse is gone on a break but only for a few minutes." He was already pushing me in the chair. We went through the ward to the elevator, onto the elevator, down a busy hall, past reception, then outside. Uncle Isaac was there waiting for us. Between the two of them they lifted me up and put me in the cab.

"Hey!" the driver objected. "What's going on?"

"A buck tip says you don't care," Uncle Isaac answered. "Don't worry. We aren't kidnapping the kid. This is his dad. The kid just don't want to be in the hospital no more."

"Hey, sonny, is that right?"

"Yes," I said.

"Well, who does?" the cabby said. We drove off. "Maybe the bill's been left unpaid too."

"Bill's been paid," Uncle Isaac said. "The doc just wanted him to stay longer. But make it two bucks."

"Two it is," agreed the cab driver.

I slumped against Father. And slept again, but not before I said, "I'm glad you came. I'm glad you came."

"You can count on me," Father said. "Just remember that."

Chapter Fifteen

We couldn't go back to the same hotel now that authorities at the hospital knew where to find us. We went to another hotel, this one near a big park and the ocean. Father helped me change my clothes in the cab so that when I got out I wouldn't attract any attention. We got up to the room, which had two double beds. Father got me undressed again and tucked me in, like I was a baby.

When I woke up it was dark. Father was reading, sitting in a chair under a lamp.

"Uncle Isaac has gone to get some food," Father said. "How are you?"

"I feel better," I said.

Just then Uncle Isaac bustled in. He put a large glass of milk on the table beside me as well as a container of chicken soup and some applesauce.

"It's all soft food," he said. "Should be easy on your neck, in case it's hard to swallow."

It hurt a bit but not too much. And I was hungry. I ate everything.

Father told me to go back to sleep. I didn't think I could, but after a trip to the bathroom down the hall I was exhausted again, and before I knew it I was waking up and it was morning.

The days ran into one another as I ate and slept and walked around the hotel room a bit, until I finally started to get bored. Father said that was a good sign, and he let me get dressed so we could go outside for a walk. It was a sunny day and the park beside the hotel was crowded. It was so beautiful. The mountains rose out of the water across the bay. The trees were green and flowers were in bloom everywhere, a riot of purple, red, yellow and pink. I bent over a bed of pink snapdragons and blue violets and red poppies. I just stared at them for a while as if seeing them for the first time. They looked bright and shiny. I glanced up to see children frolicking in the water and young men and women swimming off a long dock.

"We're going home soon," Father said.

"How?" I asked.

"Uncle Isaac has been in touch with people here at Jewish Services. They want to help us. They don't want to see us sent back to Germany. They are furious with their government. Apparently Canada won't let in *any* Jews from Europe. *None.* In fact that's what the immigration director said: 'None is too many.' So they don't care if they have to break the law to help us."

He paused. "You know, we couldn't even be citizens here. All Germans and Italians lost their citizenship in 1940. One day they were Canadians; the next day they weren't."

"It's worse here than in Seattle, you mean," I said quietly, knowing he was telling me all this for a reason.

"That's right, yes. And worse for Uncle Isaac too, should he be caught. At least at home he's a citizen. He has rights. He's coming with us."

"Really?"

"Yes. He hasn't been gone that long. His trial won't be for another month. They don't know he's even been out of the country."

"You convinced him, didn't you?"

"Yes."

"Why?"

"Because otherwise he'll spend his whole life on the run. It's time for him to stop all this and settle down. Marry. Have a family. Even if he has to serve a short term in prison, he'll come out and the business will be there and he'll be okay. And no more gambling!"

I was tired when we got back to our room. Uncle Isaac was waiting for us.

"There's a car downstairs," he said. "We're going now."

"What's happened?" Father asked.

"The folks at Jewish Services have heard that the border crossings are to be watched more

closely. They think we'd better go now. They
want to drive us to a place where they hope it'll be
safe to cross. It's farther inland and it'll take a few
hours to get there. It'll mean a longer trip back to
Seattle, but they think we should just get across
the border safely and worry about the rest later.
I've packed up your knapsack, Ben. And I've got
our things ready too."

"I'm not sure Ben is up to it yet," Father said.

"I'm fine," I assured him. "And soon we'll be
home so Mother can fuss over me."

He raised his eyebrows. Was I telling him I
wouldn't run away again? I hadn't decided yet.
Ever since Father stood over my bed and told me
he'd never let me down, something in my head
seemed to have changed.

Maybe I'd been wrong. Maybe Uncle Isaac
was right when he said that at least our family was
still together. And it was Father who had done all
that. On the other hand, if they suddenly decided
to round us up the way they did John and his
family, how could I stop them? I'd just be there
like a sitting duck. I was too afraid of that. So I
didn't know anymore; I wasn't sure. But for now,
I decided it was best to go with Father because
being in Vancouver was certainly no better than
being in Seattle. And Father needed to get home
to Mother and Marta.

We went outside, where a driver in a big black
car was waiting for us. Uncle Isaac sat in front

with him. The driver was a young man, cheerful. He chatted away with Uncle Isaac.

We drove inland. I fell asleep at some point and woke up feeling groggy. The sun was setting when the driver pulled up at what looked like the middle of nowhere.

"There's a small trail there." He pointed. "Stick to it. It'll lead into a larger path that eventually meets up with a farmer's field. Cross the field, keeping the trees on your left. Once across you'll be in the United States, and you can hitch a ride to Seattle. Good luck."

Father and Uncle Isaac thanked him and shook his hand.

"Glad to help," he said. "We don't want to send any more Jews back to Hitler."

We started to walk, following his directions. It was almost dark. Fortunately the highway was empty of cars, but nonetheless we hurried to get away from it as quickly as possible. Then Uncle Isaac spotted a police car pulling up on the highway, and he hissed, "Run!" We were well on our way down the path already, and running took us to the larger path within half a minute. Uncle Isaac dropped his suitcase. Father dropped my knapsack. I could barely keep up with them, I was still so weak. How did the police find us? Chance? Or were we being followed? Could that cabbie from the hospital have told them what hotel we were at? But wouldn't they have picked us up before? All this rushed through my head as I tried not to trip, tried not to look back. I could hear the police shouting, "Stop! Stop!" I could see the farmer's field ahead. Uncle Isaac and Father had their arms around my back. A shot was fired. Birds flew into the air and shrieked.

"We're not stopping," Father said. "Let them shoot. No stopping. Hitler'll kill us anyway. Can't stop."

We kept going. Halfway across the field another shot hit a tree right beside us. We scrambled down a small ravine. On the other side there was a road.

"Which way?" Father panted.

Uncle Isaac looked up at the sky. "That way. West."

I glanced back. There were two forms standing in the field, but no more shots. We must have been over the border.

Father had surprised me. I thought he'd turn us in, not take a chance of our being shot. But he hadn't. He hadn't.

Finally we sank down by the side of the road. I was almost fainting and I was dying of thirst. We waited and waited for a car but none came. When one finally did, it didn't stop.

It was cold. We huddled together. There was nothing to do but wait until morning.

Chapter Sixteen

I was shivering. Father and Uncle Isaac were asleep, slumped by the side of the road. Suddenly a huge figure appeared in front of me. I turned to Father.

"Wake up." He didn't move.

"Uncle Isaac. Wake up!"

He lay still, as if unconscious.

I shook Father. He slept on.

The figure must have been ten feet tall and dressed in a long tunic and loose pants. The clothes looked brown one moment, yellow another and then almost gold the next.

I leapt up, ready to fight. But then I wondered if I were dreaming because once I was standing, the figure wasn't big anymore; it was just about my size. A man, I thought, although for some reason it was hard to tell. It was dark out—very dark—the moon only a sliver in the sky.

"What do you want?" I asked.

"What do *you* want?"

"Look, I don't want trouble, that's for sure. But I'll fight you if I have to."

"Isn't that what you're doing already? Come on. I'm here to fight. You've been calling me."

"You're crazy. I haven't been calling you. I don't even know you."

"That's true. You don't know me at all. But you think you do. Come on. Let's fight."

He took a swipe at me. I ducked. Should I run? Why wouldn't Father and Uncle Isaac wake up?

"Have you hurt my father? Why won't he wake up?"

"This is between you and me," he said. "Come on, fight." He took another swipe.

I ducked again, and then I grabbed for his shoulders to see if I could throw him to the ground. He eluded my grasp but managed to trip me. I fell over, landed with a jolt on my side, shot my hand out, grabbed his ankle and pulled as hard as I could. He fell too. We grappled, each trying to pin the other. I saw the flash of a blade. I looked at my thigh and saw blood oozing through my pants. I couldn't believe it. Not again! I lunged at him, managing to knock the knife away. He grabbed at it. I got up. I started to run. He came after me. I was limping because of my wound and couldn't run fast. He got closer and closer. I turned and faced him. Closer. I threw myself at him, figuring I'd rather die fighting than with a knife in my back.

I grabbed him and threw him to the ground. I pinned him down. The knife fell away.

"Give up," I said.

"Choose life," he said.

"What?"

"Choose life."

I was flooded by a feeling of peace. Calm. And something else I couldn't name, something I hadn't experienced since before all the trouble started in Germany. It was so strange. I'd forgotten. Forgotten...

"Ben! Ben. We've got a ride. Come on, son."

My eyes flew open. Where was I? What was happening?

Father was pulling me up off the ground. We were still on the road. The sun was coming up. An old car was dead ahead. I looked at my leg. No blood. No wound. No cut at all.

I followed Father to the car.

"Hello." A middle-aged fellow was behind the wheel. "Get in."

Uncle Isaac sat in front with him. Father and I sat in the back.

Father looked at me. "You're shaking."

"Am I?" I said, teeth chattering.

"There's a blanket on the floor there," the man said over his shoulder. "Wrap the boy up. You been out all night?"

"We were visiting and got lost," Uncle Isaac

said. "We just need to get to the nearest town so we can catch a bus to Seattle."

"No problem," the man said. "The bus goes in every morning at ten. I'll drop you at the café."

Father wrapped me up in the blanket, but I couldn't stop shaking. A dream. Had I been dreaming? I'd never had a dream so real.

"You're crying," Father said quietly.

I was remembering that feeling. It was so beautiful. I'd forgotten anything could be beautiful. Forgotten how it felt. I was surrounded by darkness. By evil.

I closed my eyes. But I couldn't stop crying.

"That boy all right?" the man asked.

"He's tired," Father said. "He's upset from being outside all night."

"What he needs is some good food," the man said. "Look, my farm's just up here. Mother always makes a large breakfast for the family and the hired hands. Come on, have some breakfast with us."

"No, we couldn't," Father said.

"Bus isn't till ten. It's right up here. That boy needs warming up."

Uncle Isaac looked at Father. Father nodded.

"Thank you, sir," Uncle Isaac said. "That's very kind of you."

We pulled into a long driveway.

"We do all sorts here," he said. "Vegetables mostly. And chickens. Eggs."

The house was a long low affair, very neat. As soon as we got out of the car, the smell of fresh coffee and apple pie hit me. I was famished. I hadn't had a bite since the previous morning.

"My name is Gus," the man said. He called ahead. "Elizabeth, we have guests."

Elizabeth. I stopped for a moment. Instead of the horrible feeling of sadness, even despair, I always got when I heard her name, I was flooded with memories of my Elizabeth. Our talks. Our jokes. Our laughter. I remembered my Elizabeth and it made me feel happy to remember her. The memory wasn't surrounded by agony. Why? What was happening to me?

His wife came to the door. She was a big woman with thick grayish hair pulled back in a bun. "Visitors?" she said. "Come on then. It'll get cold." We followed Gus and Elizabeth into the house. The front room was filled with people— two young women, with babies and small children around them, three young men, two older men—all sitting at a long table.

We sat down at the end of the table. Plates were put in front of us, piled high with eggs, meat pies and fresh bread. I was given a glass of hot coffee and told to drink it down. The food was delicious. Everyone was talking at once. The babies were crying. The adults were discussing the crops and who was doing what work, and then the older children had to get ready for school and Gus said he'd take us to the bus.

Father thanked Elizabeth. "I'm happy to do God's work," she answered.

I looked up at her, shocked.

"What's the matter, sonny?" she asked.

"Is this God's work?" I blurted out.

"Be kind to strangers. Remember how Abraham invited strangers to eat with him? All through the Bible, God shows us it's our Christian duty to feed the stranger."

"I'm not Christian," I said.

"Well, I can tell from your father's accent you aren't from around here. Doesn't matter to me."

"We're Jewish," I said.

"Well then, you're God's chosen, aren't you? More reason to be good to you."

"Would you do it if God didn't tell you?"

She threw her head back and laughed, and then she looked at my father. "He's quite a character, your boy." She turned back to me. "Silly question. He did tell us."

"Come on," Gus said, "you'll miss your bus."

We got into the car. Gus said, "Sounds like your boy has a lot on his mind."

"We escaped Hitler," Father explained. "It hasn't been easy."

"Now that man is just plain evil," Gus said. "Me, I think we should've gone to war years ago, not waited this long. After all, if they'd beat

England, where would we be? No, we didn't need that attack on Pearl Harbor to get us into this war. We did it all wrong. No one likes to get involved if it isn't their fight, but we're all brothers and sisters. It's our fight, all right. We found that out too late." He shook his head.

I didn't understand. Had these people been around all along? Nice people who weren't out to get me, out to get us? Why hadn't I seen them before? Why was I seeing them now?

Chapter Seventeen

Mother didn't cry when I came home. She kissed me. "I love you, Ben," she said, "but I'm fed up with you. It's time you started to think about other people, not just yourself."

I started to tell her that all I'd done was try to get them to see sense, but there was a look on her face that warned me it would be best to keep quiet.

Later, when we'd eaten and were settled for the night, Marta sat on my bed and talked to me.

"Why do you hate everything, Ben?" she said.

"I don't."

"Yes, you do. You've hardly said a word to me since we've been here. It's like I'm a stranger to you."

I stared at her. She was right. She'd barely registered on me since we left Berlin. "But I'm trying to save the whole family," I protested. "I'm the only one who sees the danger we're in."

"You think Mom and Dad would let anything happen to us?"

"They couldn't help Oma or Opa," I said.

"But they've taken care of us, haven't they?" she insisted. "You have to admit that." She picked up her baseball glove and turned it over and over. "You're so busy being a know-it-all, you can't even see how much you don't know. You don't see how things really are. You're just crazy."

She was perfectly serious. Somehow, my little sister sitting there and telling me that I was nuts struck me as funny and I started to laugh. That startled her more than anything.

She patted my arm. "Boy, Ben, I was starting to think you'd forgotten how to laugh."

The next morning Mother handed me the front page of the *Seattle Times* to read.

"I know this will upset you, Ben, but it's time for us to accept what is happening."

The headline screamed:

Millions Driven To Ghettos

Adolf Hitler's agents, in the most terrible persecution in modern history, have killed at least 200,000 Jews in Russia, Poland and the Baltic States, and driven millions from their homes into medieval ghettos.

Foreign correspondents in Germany were never able to get exact figures on the dead, for they were killed so indiscriminately that no

*records were kept. Thousands lie in unmarked
graves, even in mass graves they were forced to
dig before the firing squads of S.S. troops cut
them down.*

*Hitler, on January 30, 1939, declared
another world war would result in destruction
of the Jews, and correspondents who live in
Germany know that he and his agents have
done everything possible to make the prophecy
come true.*

All my worst fears, all true. The things the
Jewish papers had been reporting, but that no
one believed.

"I'm going to volunteer at the synagogue,"
Mother said. "There's a war-bond drive on and
the women are helping to raise money for it.
I have to help get rid of this monster. Maybe
you should start to focus your hatred where it
belongs."

Isn't that what I'd been doing?

At lunch I checked in with Mr. Leahy. He seemed
glad to see me back at school.

Martin came over.

"Been sick?" he asked.

"Sort of," I replied.

"What happened to your ear?"

"I got attacked," I answered.

"Wow!"

Everyone had to look. It seemed I was a celebrity all of a sudden.

"Can you start training again soon?" Mr. Leahy asked.

"I could start today. My father said just not to do too much."

"Take about five laps, see how you are."

"If it wasn't for my training," I said to him, "I might not have been able to get away. Thanks."

He nodded and patted my back. "Just glad to have you back, son."

I felt like crying again. Instead I took an easy jog around the track. Martin caught up to me afterward. "Tonight's our meeting at the ice-cream parlor. Looks like you could use a few extra pounds."

"I'll see you there," I said.

"Good."

Why did I think he was out to get me before? He seemed pretty straightforward. If they were out to get me, the only way to find out was to go, so after school I walked over to the ice-cream parlor.

Craig was sitting in a booth. "Ben, over here! Have a seat. Glad you could make it. We like to stick together on the team."

Martin, Steven, Colin and Paul joined us, all squeezing into the one booth. Everyone ordered something different.

"Get the banana split," Martin suggested.

I ordered it. It was the most amazing thing I'd ever tasted: whipped cream and three different flavors of ice cream, nuts, chocolate and half a banana on either side with a big juicy cherry on the top.

"Good, huh?" Martin said with a grin.

After a while I started to relax because it seemed they weren't out to get me after all. I'd been wrong about them. Was I wrong about anything else? I was so confused. Did I dare trust Father? Did I dare relax, even for a moment?

After I left them I walked over to John's house. I was horrified to find that I must have left the door unlocked when I last left. And I had promised to take care of their place. Fortunately no one had been squatting, but the house looked terrible— dust everywhere, one of the windows cracked from a falling branch, the yard and garden overgrown with weeds. I told myself that I'd come back on the weekend to do a true cleanup. I wouldn't have time until then because Mother had made me say yes to seeing the rabbi about being bar mitzvahed. I'd agreed in a moment of weakness, when I was feeling bad about running off.

Mother was waiting outside, so I was able to be frank with Rabbi Ludwig.

"I'm not sure I want to do this."

"Why not?"

"I don't believe in God. Or maybe I do and I don't like Him."

"These times can be very trying to one's faith," Rabbi Ludwig agreed, his manner mild, not at all upset by what I'd said. "But you don't need to believe in God to have a bar mitzvah—at least not in a Reform *shul*. You just need to be Jewish and thirteen. It's a time-honored ritual, Ben, as much for your family as for you—the symbolic day you become a man and leave boyhood behind."

I thought for a minute. That didn't sound too bad. And since I'd been home I'd been feeling pretty crummy about how I had made Mother and Father worry. This might make it up to them a little.

"All right," I said. "I guess we can talk about what I'd need to do."

"I've been looking at the portions you could read," Rabbi Ludwig said. "It'll take us a while to prepare...probably until November. That will take us up to Jacob and the story of his battle with an angel. It'll be too hard for you to do it in Hebrew. I think if you can read it in English, that will be enough of a challenge for you. And we like the bar mitzvah boy to give a small talk about the portion we are reading that week. A little speech." He paused. "Are you familiar with the story of Jacob?"

I shook my head. "We studied some Bible stories at Hebrew school, but I don't remember any of them very well."

"Jacob runs away from his uncle's house

into the desert," the rabbi explained. "He finds out that his brother is coming after him with an army. He's scared. He thinks Esau will kill him. He goes to sleep. And while he sleeps, an angel, perhaps God Himself, comes to him in a vision. They wrestle. Jacob finally pins the angel down and won't release him until the angel blesses him. The angel does. And he gives him the name Israel. The angel says, 'You have wrestled with God and men and prevailed.'"

The rabbi paused. "Ben?"

I couldn't speak.

"Ben, are you ill? Shall I call your mother?"

I nodded.

When Mother came in, I said, "I can't do this right now. I need to leave."

"Rabbi, can we come back another day?" my mother asked.

"Of course," he said.

I was thankful to her for not questioning me in front of him and for getting me out of there. Maybe that's why I opened up to her as we walked home. It was a longish walk, about half an hour, so we had a lot of time to talk.

I told her about the dream I'd had that night on the road and how like it was to the portion the rabbi had chosen for me to read.

She stopped walking for a moment when I'd finished, and when she started again, she seemed almost at a loss for words.

"You never really knew your other grandparents," she said finally. "Your Baba and Zaida."

Baba had died when I was three, Zaida when I was five.

"Your Baba was very spiritual. She believed in a very personal God and she had conversations with Him or His angels all the time. Sometimes it would be through dreams, sometimes when she prayed. Very much like what you're describing."

Again I didn't say anything, this time because I was stunned. Mother had never hinted at this, and she's so practical it never occurred to me that she had come from a religious family.

"How did you feel after the dream?" she asked me. "Different?"

I thought for a moment. "Yes. Everything seemed full of light and I felt peaceful and I felt…"

"What?"

"I don't know. Love, maybe. I felt love all around me." I paused. "I know that sounds dumb."

"That's what Baba used to say when she had one of her 'encounters,' as she used to call them. Maybe you take after her. I used to think it was all nonsense. But hearing you say almost the same things—well, it really might make a believer out of me!"

"But why would it?" I asked. "I mean, all the misery, all the hate. What's to believe in? A god that can create that?"

"Where does love come from?" Mother asked.

"I don't know."

"You must admit that if you give God credit for hate, you have to give Him credit for love," she pointed out.

"Why should I?"

"Because you need to be fair."

"Why? God isn't."

"We're talking about *you*, not God."

We stopped walking for a moment and stared at each other.

"Jacob is wounded in the thigh before he pins down the angel," Mother said. "Did you know that?"

"He is?"

"Yes."

"So was I, in my dream."

"I remember studying that passage," Mother said. "I think the wounding is interpreted to mean that you can't grow up until you suffer. You can't understand the world. That's why Adam and Eve *had* to eat from the tree of knowledge."

"*Why* should we have to suffer before we grow up? Why didn't God make the world so we could grow up without suffering?"

"How would that work? Without darkness there could be no light. Without life, no death. Without good, evil. How could we live in a world with only one dimension? Maybe that would be heaven. But how could we ever learn anything?"

"God could have made it so we don't need to learn. God makes the rules." Even as I said it, I knew that a world like that would make no sense either. You couldn't learn or grow. I thought of Oma's flowers. What would they be if they couldn't ever blossom? Was it possible that my long-dead Baba had somehow given me a gift that might help me understand this cruel world?

Mother and I walked the rest of the way home in silence, she as deep in thought as I.

Chapter Eighteen

"Ben," Marta said at breakfast, "you look different."

"Do I?"

"Yes."

"How?"

"You don't look so mad."

I smiled at her.

"You should get some friends," she advised me.

"I should?"

"Why don't you have some fun?" She looked at me for a minute. "Elizabeth would like it if you had fun. She *loved* fun."

How had she read my mind? I guess I'd somehow felt that if Elizabeth were dead, I had no right to have fun anymore. Would Elizabeth mind? Should I? Or would it be admitting that everything that happened was all right. I didn't think it was all right. I could never think that.

« »

Track practice went really well, and when we were finished we started to split up to go home. About a block from the school, Martin, Craig, Paul and I were still walking together when Bill showed up. But he wasn't alone. He had his two pals, plus the four goons, including Lester. He spoke to Martin.

"Hey, Mitchell, I got no beef with you. Why don't you and your friends get lost and leave this kike to us."

"You need someone to wash your mouth out," Martin said, his voice calm.

"And who would that be?" Bill retorted.

Paul answered. "Well, that would be the track team. You take on one of us, you take on all of us."

All kinds of thoughts raced through my mind. On the one hand, my first reaction was to tell Martin to get lost since it wasn't his fight. But Marta's words reverberated in my head. *You should get some friends.* And right now they were offering to be my friends and I did need them, because if it were just me against all these goons, I would be finished. On the other hand, if these guys really were my friends, they shouldn't have to get hurt. And there were only four of us and seven of them.

"You guys need to get out of here," I said to Martin and the others. "It's not your fight."

"It's always our fight if they take on one of us," Martin said. "Besides, even if you weren't on the team, I don't like his mouth." He said the last loud enough for Bill to hear.

Before I got a chance to respond, Bill grabbed me and swung me around, his arm around my throat so I couldn't breathe, and Lester threw a punch right into my stomach. I would have doubled over, but Bill held me upright. Martin clipped Lester on the jaw, and Lester dropped. I could feel Bill's grip loosen just a bit. I squirmed under his arm and jabbed him hard, hitting him in his side so he let me go.

I'm not sure what happened next, but something took me over and Bill could have been wearing a Nazi Youth uniform. I was just so sick of guys like him—bullies and people full of hate—that I started punching and hitting, and once he was down I went for the others. It was as if I had the strength of ten men and I wanted to use it all to hurt Bill and his buddies. I wanted to kill them. I wanted to wipe them off the face of the earth so there wouldn't be any more bad people, and if God wouldn't do it, I'd do it for Him...

"Ben! Ben! Stop it. They're done. Stop." Martin was holding on to me. I looked around. Bill, Lester and the rest were all down, groaning, trying to get up, blood everywhere.

There was blood trickling down my chin from a cut on my lip. Martin already had a black eye. Paul looked fresh as a daisy, but I knew he'd fought. He was quick. He was helping Craig up. Craig was holding his stomach.

"You okay?" Martin asked me.

"Are you?" I asked him.

"Just fine." He grinned.

I turned to Paul and Craig. "You fellows all right?"

Paul said, "These guys have had it coming a long time."

Craig agreed. "I've seen them go after the Japanese. Made me sick."

And then we walked away from those goons as if we couldn't even be bothered to give them the time of day.

"Thanks," I said as we walked.

"You'd do the same for us," Martin said.

With a shock I realized that he was right. I would.

We said good-bye, but I couldn't go home. I needed to think. I headed over to John's house.

I went inside. The bare floors were covered with dust. I sank down on the floor, my back against the wall.

And that brings me to today, to the empty house, to revisiting and rethinking it all. And after all that thinking, what do I know? Do I know anything for sure? Do I understand anything?

One thing does jump out at me, out of this whirlwind of tiny pieces of my life—every memory, every slice of film, is about *me*. It's normal, I guess, for me to be the hero of my own movie, but there should be supporting players, even players with equal billing. But everyone except me seems to be almost invisible. Marta said that to me and she was right, not just about herself but also about everyone else. The track team, John—supposedly my best friend—even Mother and Father are like shadow figures, hardly defined, barely there. Only I matter in my movie. That can't be right. And when we lived in Germany, before we were thrown out of school, it wasn't like that. But after that, I don't know, somehow it changed. And surely I'm no worse off than a soldier fighting the Nazis, or the Jews left behind, or John, stuck in a camp.

Suddenly I sense I am not alone. Maybe someone has been squatting at the house after all. I look up. Sure enough, someone is standing in the middle of the room. I am so tired and confused that I can't be bothered to be scared. If he wants to kill me, I won't fight. He's tall. Dressed in some sort of loose pants and long shirt. I can't see his face. He seems to be in shadow, although there's plenty of light coming in through the windows; dust motes float through the air, swirling in the shafts of sunlight.

"I won't hurt you," he says. His voice is sweet and melodious. I've heard it before—that day on the road!

"Who are you, anyway?" I ask.

"Who do you think I am?"

"How should I know?"

"If you don't know, then who does?"

"Am I dreaming?"

"What do you think?"

"I don't know."

"Well, if you don't, who does?"

"Actually," I say, exasperated, "you just might be God, like the rabbi said. I mean, you're *annoying* enough to be God."

"Why do you say that?"

"Answering a question with another question. Why can't you be brave enough to answer, really answer? Tell me what is going on. Explain the rules."

"What rules?"

"See? There you go again."

"You're right. Ask me something else. I'll see what I can do."

"Why didn't God make the world so there would be no suffering?"

"How would that work?"

"Hey. You promised."

My visitor laughs. A wonderful sound, like birds singing in the morning.

"Without darkness, how could there be light? Without life, death. Without good, evil. Isn't that what everyone tells you? Because those are words you understand. What if there is no such thing as good and evil? In some places people think dancing is evil. In other places it's considered a wonderful thing. What if it is all up to you to decide? What if even life and death aren't what you think they are?"

"You mean we don't really die."

"You are here because you choose to be."

"Choice. That's all I hear."

"That's all there is."

"That's all?"

"Well, there's something else."

"What?"

"Love."

I jump up. Mad. "Love. That's fine for you to say. If you loved people you would make sure they didn't suffer."

"Don't you think that's up to you?"

A loud knocking jolts me. Suddenly the room is empty. Someone is knocking at the front door. I hurry over. It is an old lady, white haired and stooped. "What are you doing here? This is the Ogawas' house."

"I'm here to look after it," I say. "I'm a friend of John's. I was checking to see if anything needs to be done."

"It certainly does, young fellow," she says.

"I'll come back on Saturday," I promise, "and get it all cleared up."

"You do that," she says approvingly. "I'll come over and help you with the garden."

I shut the door and look around. In the middle of the room there are footprints in the dust. Mine? Or the visitor's? I can't tell. They're the same size as mine. But there are no others around it. Was God talking to me? Or is it just my imagination?

Does it matter which it is?

After supper, Father sits at the kitchen table.

"I'm almost finished the translation of Job," he announces. "It was useful for me. A help for my English and it certainly makes you think. Job endures everything thrown at him. He argues with God and calls Him out but never curses Him or blames Him." He looks at me. "I'm at the part where God finally speaks to Job out of the whirlwind. What do you think that means? What is the whirlwind?"

"Is it like a storm?" I ask.

"Yes, it could also be translated as tempest. I wonder, though, why wouldn't God speak out of a place of peace? Of love?"

"I'm not sure," I say slowly, trying to figure that out. "My mind feels like a whirlwind all the time, with thoughts and feelings and arguments swirling round and round. Do you think that's what it means? That all of creation—God, us, even the Nazis—is full of everything—good, evil…"

Father continues. "Love, fear…"

"Because if we're all made up of everything,

well, that makes sense to me," I continue, suddenly feeling very excited because I'm onto something; it's like a light going on over my head. "Hitler thinks the opposite so maybe that's right, because I *know* Hitler is wrong."

"What do you mean?" Father asks.

"Hitler thinks people are either bad or good—pure like Aryans or impure like Jews. You're either on his side or you're on the wrong side. If he saw people as all the same, full of good *and* bad, he couldn't want to hurt anyone."

Father stares at me. "You've been doing some thinking."

"I have. I don't think I want to be angry anymore. Except," I add, "at those who deserve it. Except when it can do some good. Maybe it's time to start doing something, like Mother says."

Father puts his hand over mine. "I love you, Benjamin," he says.

"I love you too," I say, surprising myself.

Father translates, "'Therefore I will be quiet and give in, being but dust and ashes.' And that's the last thing Job says."

"Why does he give up?" I ask.

"Is he giving up?" Father asks. "What are we in the end?"

"Dust," I reply. "So maybe he's accepting the world as it is."

"Maybe he is," says Father.

« »

I take a broom, a bucket and a mop over to John's house, along with writing paper and a pen. And I slip something else into my pocket.

First I clean up the old branches and leaves around the porch and house. Then I sweep the porch clean. Then I go over to the old lady's house and she lets me fill the bucket with water. I mop down the entire house.

Finally I start on the garden. I know mostly which are weeds and which are flowers, and I remember Oma as I do it and it makes me feel peaceful. And then I take out the packet of seeds she gave me the last time I saw her. As I plant the seeds in John's garden, I say a little prayer for Oma and Opa and Elizabeth. I promise them that I will never forget them.

The old lady, whose name is Mrs. Mallow, invites me over for lunch and feeds me chicken and apple pie. I like her. She has three grandsons fighting in the war.

When everything is done, I sit on the porch steps and write my letter to John.

Dear John,

Thank you for your letter. I'm sorry I haven't written before. I haven't been very well. I've been upset and angry. I ran away twice. But I don't want to be so angry anymore. I don't want to be full of fear and hatred. I hope you aren't feeling too bitter. I wouldn't blame you. But it doesn't help.

*Well, maybe it helps to get mad so that
you can try to change things. I still want to
fight Hitler. I still hate him. I want to fight
everyone here on earth who is bad. I'm going
back to work selling papers, but I'm going to
give all my money to war bonds.*

*I know that this is a strange letter to get
from me. We never spoke of these things. But
as my friend, I hope you will understand.*

*I know you've been following baseball.
Did you see that Paul Waner got his three
thousandth hit off Rip Sewell? And did you
read that he actually got it a couple of days
ago, but it bounced off Eddie Joost's glove
and he didn't think that was a clean hit so he
convinced the ump to call it an error? Since
the Dodgers are your team, they'll be mine too,
although are you sure you don't want to root
for the Yankees? I like Di Maggio. No, you're
probably right. And the Dodgers sometimes
come out west, so maybe we could see them
sometime.*

Your friend,

Ben

*P.S. I'm going to see if Father will come
with me to visit you. Would you like me to
bring anything? I'd be happy to bring whatever
you or your family needs.*

*P.P.S. I'm sorry it's taken me so long to
write.*

Carol Matas is an internationally acclaimed author of over thirty-five novels for children and young adults. Her best-selling work, which includes three award-winning series, has been translated into many languages.

Carol has won many awards including the Geoffrey Bilson Award, the inaugural Silver Birch Award and the Jewish Book Award. Her books have appeared on numerous honor lists, such as the ALA notable list, the *New York Times* notable list and the New York Public Library list of books for the Teen Age. She has also been nominated twice for a Governor General's Literary Award. Carol lives in Winnipeg, Manitoba, with her husband.

More information about Carol is available on her website: www.carolmatas.com

The immigration systems in both the United States and Canada put limits or quotas on refugees during the war years. Canada's policy was to let in as few Jews as possible, declaring, "None is too many." In the United States, twenty-seven thousand Germans were allowed in per year, but for Jews the process was difficult. They needed affidavits of support from relatives or Jewish organizations in the United States. These affidavits had to guarantee the person would not be a burden on the state—and yet Jews were not allowed to take any money with them when they left Germany.

In 1937, President Franklin D. Roosevelt issued his own affidavit declaring that there was to be no limit on Jewish children allowed into the United States as long as there were homes for them. This was the exact opposite of the Canadian position. In fact, at one point, Jewish children in France whose parents had been shipped east would have been allowed to leave France if anyone had accepted them. Canada turned them away, although some did manage to make it to the United States. From 1933 to

1945, according to Abella and Troper in *None Is Too Many*, the United States allowed in two hundred thousand Jewish refugees; Canada allowed in fewer than five thousand.

The record concerning the Japanese community in both countries is a dismal one. Immediately following Japan's attack on Pearl Harbor, the FBI began arresting *Issei* (first-generation Japanese Americans) in Seattle and all along the American west coast, as well as some *Nisei* (the first generation of Japanese Americans born in the United States). The *Nisei* in Seattle wanted to contribute to the US war effort. But the government and the press whipped up the public with racist attacks, and on February 19, 1942, President Roosevelt signed Executive Order 9066. This order authorized the removal of "any or all persons" from any area considered a military zone and allowed the military to take over responsibility from the government for civilians. When the WRA or War Relocation Authority was formed, it oversaw the relocation of the Japanese. One hundred and ten thousand people were sent to internment camps and imprisoned for the rest of the war. Two-thirds of those interned were American citizens. However, many *Nisei* were accepted into the army and fought bravely for their country, even as their families remained imprisoned in these camps. The 442nd Army regiment, an all-Japanese unit, was one of the most decorated units in the war, and not one Japanese American was actually convicted of spying or helping the enemy.

Just as they did with the Jewish immigrants, Canadians treated Japanese immigrants more severely than did the Americans. Most Japanese Canadians lived in

British Columbia, and about three-quarters of those had been born in Canada or were naturalized Canadians. As in the United States, the newspapers and local politicians led the attack on their friends and neighbors. In the winter of 1942, the relocations began but in a more extreme version than in the United States. Property was confiscated.

An excellent account of this period can be found on the website JapaneseCanadianHistory.net (2005). The following excerpt is used with the kind permission of Masako Fukawa, Project Leader. Thank you also to Reiko Tagami of the Japanese Canadian National Museum for facilitating the use of the information from this website and for fact-checking the historical note.

The order in 1942, to leave the "restricted area" and move 100 miles inland from the west coast was made under the authority of the War Measures Act and affected over 21,000 Japanese Canadians. Most were first held in the livestock barns in Hasting Park (Vancouver's Pacific National Exhibition grounds) and then moved to hastily built camps in the BC interior. At first, many men were separated from their families and sent to road camps in Ontario and on the BC/Alberta border. Small towns in the BC interior such as Greenwood, Sandon, New Denver and Slocan became internment quarters mainly for women, children and the aged. To stay together, some families agreed to work on sugar beet farms in Alberta and Manitoba where there were labour shortages. Those who resisted and challenged the orders of the Canadian government were rounded up by the RCMP *and incarcerated in a barbed-wire prisoner-of-war camp in Angler, Ontario.*

Despite earlier government promises to the contrary, the Custodian of Enemy Alien Property sold the confiscated property. The proceeds were used to pay auctioneers and realtors, and to cover storage and handling fees. The remainder paid for the small allowances given to those in internment camps. Unlike prisoners of war of enemy nations who were protected by the Geneva Convention, Japanese Canadians were forced to pay for their own internment. Their movements were restricted and their mail censored.

As World War II was drawing to a close, Japanese Canadians were strongly encouraged to prove their "loyalty" by "moving east of the Rockies" immediately or signing papers agreeing to be "repatriated" to Japan when the war was over. Many moved to the Prairie provinces, Ontario and Quebec. About 4,000, half of them Canadian born, were exiled in 1946 to Japan. Prime Minister Mackenzie King declared in the House of Commons on August 4, 1944: "It is a fact no person of Japanese race born in Canada has been charged with any act of sabotage or disloyalty during the years of war."

On April 1, 1949, four years after the war was over, all the restrictions were lifted and Japanese Canadians were given full citizenship rights, including the right to vote and the right to return to the west coast. But there was no home to return to. The Japanese Canadian community in British Columbia was virtually destroyed.

Recommended books on the plight of "enemy aliens" during World War II

Abella, Irving and Harold Troper, *None Is Too Many*, Lester and Orpen Dennys, Toronto, 1982.

Cole, Molly, Howard Droker and Jacqueline Williams, *Family of Strangers: Building a Jewish Community in Washington State*, Washington State Jewish Historical Society, Seattle, in association with University of Washington Press, 2003.

Miki, Roy and Cassandra Kobayashi, *Justice in Our Time*, Talonbooks, 1991.

Oppenheim, Joanne, *Dear Miss Breed*, Scholastic Press, 2006.

Takami, David A., *Divided Destiny: A History of Japanese-Americans in Seattle*. University of Washington Press, 1998.

Warren, James, *The War Years, A Chronicle of Washington State in World War II*, History Ink, University of Washington Press, 2000.

Webpage
http://japanesecanadianhistory.net/the_war_years.htm